Sir Phoebus's Ma

Sir Phoebus's Ma

ZÖE TEALE

PHOENIX HOUSE
LONDON

First published in Great Britain in 1995
by Phoenix House
Orion House,
5 Upper St Martin's Lane
London WC2H 9EA

The line on p.1 from *Novel on Yellow Paper*, 1936, by Stevie
Smith, is reproduced by kind permission of Virago Press Ltd.

The line on p.94 is from *The Years*, 1937, by Virginia Woolf.

A CIP catalogue record for this book is
available from the British Library

ISBN 1 89758 0 57 6
1 89758 0 62 2

Typeset at The Spartan Press Ltd,
Lymington, Hants

Printed in Great Britain by Butler & Tanner Ltd
Frome and London

*For Lettice Lane,
and for my parents
on their fiftieth birthdays*

Prologue

I guess what was wanted was a human story and not wise-cracks about the habits of the natives, which would not come too well anyway from Sir Phoebus's ma.

Stevie Smith

We walk into town at the usual brisk-to-put-it-nicely pace, me skipping every fourth stride to catch up, Moriya sensei marching with his head held up to the clouds. We pass the French bakery and he goes in to get some rolls, comes out clutching a bottle of Beaujolais nouveau and some tiramisu-flavoured donuts.

'So where's the party?' I humour him, because it is a sunny day and I slept well. He looks overjoyed at this scrap of warmth – stutters, 'Shall we go and have a you know what?'

And for once I don't play dense.

'Mitsukoshi fruit juice?'

But he seems to be in an even greater hurry now. He is spinning down Ichibancho like a hurricane, and people scatter before his wild arms, until – hitting a young man, crashing against the staggering body – he is stilled. The glasses leap from his face. The two men grope around on the pavement, clutching their heads. I stand watching Mr Moriya blind and on his knees.

We take the elevator to the ground floor of Mitsukoshi and note that the attendants have changed from summer yellow uniforms into dark suits with pill-box hats. The woman flops her forearm down to show we are descending into the food hall. Today in the fruit bar there are rather fewer flavours on display than usual and I choose fresh strawberry. They are also selling enormous apples with pictures on the skin – pictures made with stencils while the fruit is ripening. The price is so high that I laugh.

He is certainly in a hurry to go.

We get to the underground and head off into the suburbs, then take the bus and walk up the lane.

He calls his wife from the doorway, but the house looks very empty to me, and he seems to be acting his surprise that she is not

3

in. My heart leaps and sinks. I am quite, quite sure that this has been planned.

'Well,' he says, looking over his shoulder. 'I don't know where she's got to but come on in. I will go to my bedroom for a moment. Make yourself comfortable in our daughter's room. Why don't you change into *kimono*?'

I come through the doorway and take my shoes off slowly. The house is very silent, and he is breathing, I think, a little more heavily than normal. But I don't think anything will happen. I just feel that he is somehow getting a kick from our being alone, with no one else even in shouting distance. If that's all he wants – does he deserve my hatred or my fear for this? Does he deserve such effort? For we are still here, playing the same old circular games that we have played now month after month.

I do not change. I don't even want to be in the bedroom. Instead I go to the kitchen, where I cannot feel his presence at all. I open the refrigerator and spend a long time choosing something to drink, and then I contemplate the glasses. There is some pumpkin tempura left on a plate and I eat a piece which is so good that it momentarily distracts me from thinking of him. I look for the soy sauce and have a second piece dipped in that. Then I pour out the drink.

I can hear him moving about his room, and then he is still. My back muscles are alert, but in my head I know that he will never actually harm me physically. This is not a physical battle. But I am left with questions I cannot answer – for I can never know beyond doubt what he is thinking. Even now it is possible that I am making all of this up. Possible that there is only me in the battle. Or is it a simple error of translation, a misunderstanding? A jest? This is my daily liturgy, for I am unable to ignore him – I watch, I live by him, scathing yet fascinated.

It is difficult to say when these feelings first began to root themselves, to build upon each other – possibly it was long before I met him, the old woodwork teacher who laid his hands each week on mine to show me how to use the plane or the polisher, the tutor who smiled slily as he said he admired innocence, making me shift in my armchair. From that first evening, as he told me how he had 'ordered' me from the prefectural office, asking for three things, his voice and his movements began to clot and harden in me.

Others can say the same and yet mean nothing. Other words disperse immediately, so that I do not even remember that they have been said. With him it was different, though whether that was me or him – really it was from our combining.

It started like a grain of sand in a shell which becomes a pearl, only mine was not a pearl but more like a cancer. Every movement that he made, every comment, seemed to be drawn into that hard area, and all my thinking was spent on it, all the energy that I had was there, fighting this cancer, and yet through concentrating on the hardness the area became harder still. Happier thoughts, happier encounters, dispersed and were lost while I was watching, guarding against him.

And all the time he was inside me.

His roots grew firmly.

He distracted me – not him precisely, but what we had made between us. Only I do blame him. He had hopes, certainly, of a special relationship which was founded on the gaps in my knowledge from the beginning. He was subtle, behind his blundering – real physical blundering belongs to the man with a sad face unbuttoning his trousers along the Path of Philosophy.

I pitied his blundering, and it distracted my attention, enabling him to enter me the more easily, again and again.

Some days when I recalled these scenes they seemed less heavy than at other times. The comings and goings are hard to explain. It was a very hot August, and a hot autumn all through – the mosquitoes would throb against my window each night, and he would throb beside me in the day.

When Aki told me about her baby while we overlooked a sea of stones one day, I saw briefly the image of these things before me, and saw how I had bound myself up in my own careful embroidery, intricate as Joseph's coat, but a winding sheet all the same. Since then, I have been trying to lay the pictures bare again, so that I may leave them or remake them as I choose. I suppose this is the reason though tomorrow, as you know, the reason might be different.

Summer

All the foreigners were on one side of the room and all the Japanese on the other. We sat through the speeches by prefectural officials. The Mayor joked about women having all the power in Japan – 'Oh yes, I have to ask my wife when I want money to go out drinking!'

'And how often does his wife go out drinking?' I asked the person next to me.

James, whom I later found to be a staunch supporter of Bush and not so keen a feminist, lifted one side of his mouth into a diplomatic smile.

Finally the speeches were finished and the two sides of the room mingled with one another like particles in a physics experiment. An elderly man and another with a terrible squint and rather greasy hair approached me timidly. I held out my hand and nodded to their 'Anna?'

The handshakes were very different. The older of the two, Sato sensei, held without pressure. The other, Moriya sensei, clasped my hand as if I would save him from a shipwreck.

'Shall we go and have a bite to eat?' asked Moriya sensei, squinting so energetically that I felt I should not look him in the face. 'Some luncheon?' I implied that I was impressed by his English and he looked flattered.

'I was in England for some time, you see. Two months in fact. In Norwich.'

'We call him the Great Englishman. You wait and see,' grinned Sato sensei.

We went to a pretty restaurant with bamboo windows and low tables, and I caused a moment of panic by declaring that I did not eat meat. I could not bring myself to decline fish.

'I thought all English liked Roast Beef. My wife has prepared Roast Beef.'

'So why Japan?' asked Sato sensei, filling the brief question out with a belly-felt laugh which baffled me.

'Well, I wanted to try living for a bit in a different culture, and it seemed like in Japan I would be giving something in return – I mean, if I'd gone to a country – a country that had been colonised by Europeans, I would feel like I was . . .'

Moriya sensei was fiddling with a spoon and it fell off the table taking some red sauce with it in an arc of colour, which cut my waffling short. I had become too serious, and now was not the time to be political.

'What do you think of Japanese people?' Mr Moriya's squint was already relaxing, the twitches coming less frequently. I thought he was the one who needed more attention and I tried to draw him out.

'And what do you think of the English?'

'Oh, Wordsworth, Shakespeare, Byron!' he cried. 'A wonderful country.'

'Ha, wonderful!' echoed Sato sensei.

'But the English today?'

'Much better than the French. Much politer. In Paris, the taxi-drivers laugh at me and slam the doors. In England they are still gentlemen. And in Scotland too.'

'Do they still wear bowler hats?' asked Sato sensei politely.

'Oh, yes, in the City. Many still do,' said Mr Moriya.

I got the impression that this little bit of praise for Old England had been run through before, that it was a game they played often. Moriya sensei's cheeks were shining.

'Sato sensei is my only friend in the school,' he confided.

Sato sensei was about to retire, so the next senior English teacher, Moriya sensei, was to be my supervisor. He invited me to come back to his home, to meet his wife and possibly stay the night. He was very thoughtful. He asked what food I liked and then made a telephone call to his wife asking her to drop the Roast Beef and prepare traditional Japanese vegetables.

The main street was in disarray owing to the Tanabata 'Star' Festival, which celebrated the reunion of two god lovers, but was famous now for its beautiful stylised paper stars – huge coloured paper from which trailed streamers and strings of origami cranes, symbols of peace.

The stars were hung from the ceiling of the covered shopping arcades and the streamers brushed our faces as we hurried to catch the train to the suburbs.

He told me over supper that I was to be their daughter, because their real daughter was living away. I was to have her room and he hoped I would come and stay as often as possible. His wife was very kind, bringing me my food – watching us as we ate. She had some plates in front of her but did not eat, not that I could see. She put the rice cooker on a mat beside the table and filled her husband's bowl – when he held out his *sake* cup she poured the invisible liquid by raising the bottom of the flask in a small curve.

After the meal he helped her carry the dishes to the kitchen, laughing that things were not as once they had been.

'Men have to help these days!'

'I should think so,' I smiled politely. I was puzzled when he tittered, put his finger to his lips.

'You are very special to me,' he said bluntly, returning, putting his legs down into the dip beneath the table. 'Do make yourself at home, you do not have to kneel.' But I was quite comfortable kneeling. I thought more so than if I put my legs down under the table with his.

'I asked the prefectural officials for three things – one, English literature graduate – two, female – three, from an old university. You were the only one who met all three conditions.'

'And why were these things so important?'

'I will tell you later why I wanted an English literature graduate. It is rather an interesting thing. The reason I did not want a man is because foreign men – sometimes I think they can be more difficult, maybe a cultural thing.'

'University?'

'Ah,' he looked, first toward the kitchen, then to me, 'because I am Romantic you see.'

*

12

At first I was fascinated – no, always, or for a long while I was that. At first it was something to write good letters home about. It was distant at the beginning.

We moved into the study, where a Union Jack covered one wall, and the cabinets were heavy with books gathered from Charing Cross Road. The Haworth parsonage linen tea towel which I had brought along with the whisky from Heathrow fitted in well here, and Mrs Moriya played the piano while we sipped wine. I went to bed quite early, and lay wide awake, allowing my mouth to relax from the day's long, forced though not unhappy smile. There were some glow-stars on the ceiling, and I imagined the daughter lying here as a child, escaping into her own small sky.

When I awoke I stayed in bed as long as possible, left it rather too long, because Moriya sensei came and knocked, asking if I was feeling okay.

At breakfast I was told the story of the stuffed pheasants displayed in the central room.

'I am terribly sorry but it is not what you think. I did not kill them myself, you understand.'

The house had once stood in a wood, only a few months ago the trees at the front had been cut down because the land was being sold to pay death duties. The house itself had been part of a much larger group of buildings once owned by the family, and it had had traditional wooden sliding doors, which, when opened, allowed house and garden, indoors and outdoors, to merge into one.

Glass windows had been added when the house was restored several years ago, but the pheasants who lived in the wood had been fooled into believing that they could still fly through the house to get to the other side. Five pheasants stunned themselves to death before the colony moved away. Now the town was advancing every day. Mr Moriya said he was beginning to feel the vibrations from the subway, and a new station closer still was being planned.

At lunch time I set off to do some shopping, and he walked

with me to the bus stop. As the bus came he grasped my hand and wrung it, forcing me to contract my palm in order to slip my fingers away.

Every lamp post dangled coloured Tanabata tassels and streamers of paper cranes linked head to foot. Along the pavements children fished at rubber ponds for goldfish, and young women in bright *kimonos* with large flowery *obi* giggled as they balanced on their wooden shoes, clutching at each other as they slipped, waving their matching bags.

I wanted to be a part of the crowd, but after shopping I had nowhere to go except my apartment. It seemed odd to have come all this way for such loneliness – to listen to old women flashing their gold teeth at jokes I did not understand. The packaging on my new kettle was so neat that I wanted to show someone, to give it to someone else to unwrap. But it was only to be seen by me.

I walked back through the University grounds where some students were singing under a tree, accompanied by a guitar. I passed the school where I was to teach, but its grey buildings were empty and a chain hung around the gate. My apartment was just along the road from the school – in a small white building called The Maisonette. Everyone was single there, sleeping in small *tatami* mat rooms, each with a bathroom and kitchen cramped in the entrance. Mr Moriya found it for me. He said I was lucky to have it because it was difficult to find places so near the centre of town.

I had been lent bedding and a television by the school until I found my own. The following day I was to meet Mr Moriya up by Mitsukoshi to go shopping for the things I couldn't carry and also for a telephone line which, he said, would be too difficult for me to negotiate.

Now I paced my apartment – on the television, as I stirred the vegetables in my frying pan, was the cartoon whose theme music had been playing in every shop I had visited – Chibi

Maruko chan – Little Chibi Maruko. She had a squeaky voice and fell asleep while helping her mother cut up vegetables. When she dreamt she floated around the sky in a little boat accompanied by a white rabbit and a magic flute player. She did not like going to school, and she cried big cartoon tears as I changed channels for the bilingual news.

We were sitting in the small office under the railway line. There was a plant, a benjamina, on the shelf behind the woman's head, and an NTT calendar on the wall with a picture of a waterfall, but apart from those only a metal desk. It did not seem very official.

I was told it was a second hand telephone line sales department, though Mr Moriya appeared confused. The woman was some kind of middleman putting people who wanted to sell telephone lines in contact with people who wanted to buy them, but Mr Moriya was whispering as if there was some sort of shady deal going on. Or possibly he was trying to appear heroic, making things seem difficult, for this fumbling could not have been necessary – he refused the woman's offer of red ink and searched through his Gladstone bag for his own, which, he told me, was better quality.

He was playing the grand samurai for me. In a café earlier he had drawn a complicated diagram in the shape of a triangle, with 'the Emperor' at the pinnacle, then 'samurai', then 'merchants', and then a nameless mass which he shaded in dark stripes but which remained unlabelled.

'Peasants,' he said with a giggle. 'And I am Samurai. That means like your Aristocracy.'

When in London he had seen women riding horses in Hyde Park, and he insisted that they must have been Noblemen's Daughters.

'I'm not sure,' I had replied once or twice already.

Certainly he was confusing the woman behind the desk. She even glanced up at me in the hope that I might tell her what was happening, but I shook my head with regret. He dropped his *hancho* and checked to make sure it had not chipped, before completing the paperwork with his stamp. The woman glanced

17

down to see if he had done everything correctly, nodded respectfully, then smiled over his head at me.

'I like this one,' I said, pointing at one of the more expensive futons. If I did not use up my allowance the money would be returned to the prefectural office, so it was like monopoly money to me. But I hated the sound of my voice, there was a coldness in it.

Moriya sensei laughed nervously and said I had good taste – he said this to the shop assistant too. 'The English always have good taste, you know.'

'Of course,' bowed the assistant.

'It would be good to have a big mirror too,' I said. 'It would make the room look bigger.'

'Ah, compared to your English rooms it is very small, I'm afraid, your room.'

'Oh no, it's a good size.' I felt embarrassed by my behaviour. I told myself I was tired.

'You see!' he said, happy immediately. 'The Englishman's room is his Palace.' He sighed, his eyes glossing over.

He was humouring me like a child, and I was being as petulant as one. I didn't feel it was for real.

'Have you visited Mitsukoshi?' he asked, and seemed disappointed that I had been there by myself.

'But have you see the mini-Harrods?'

'Real Harrods?'

'Ah, I will take you there, come. I often visit here, when I am feeling nostalgic for England.' He led me through the food hall. 'Mitsukoshi is the Japanese Harrods. In Tokyo it is very fine, very fine, like your Harrods. Here it is not so good, but everything is good quality you know.'

We came to the Harrods – a corner of teas, fruit cakes and Teddy bears with Union Jacks on their hats and dates embroidered on their feet.

'How about it?' he asked proudly. 'It will be like – how do you say it – a second home to you.' I wasn't sure what to say.

'Sometimes I buy English breakfast tea here. You want to buy anything?'

'That fruit juice looks good,' I said, pointing to the fresh juice bar over my shoulder.

'Ah, you are more interested in fruit juice than Harrods, I see, I see, let me have the honour, then. Come, choose one. What would you like? Strawberry? Kiwi?' He pulled me over to the row of stools, and I sat sipping my drink through the straw while he watched me, declining one for himself with a queenly raised hand.

A child in a sailor suit sat next to me, and her eyes kept floating up to watch me although her chin was tucked in and she pretended to be concentrating on drinking through her straw.

The day my phone was installed I sat by it hoping it would ring. It was black and a bit old fashioned, like the one we had at home ten years ago, and it made me feel comfortable – but I longed to hear its ringing. I placed it on the floor under my mirror so I could see my face reflected as I was talking to people, and then we sat together in glum silence through the whole day. Only Mr Moriya and the Headmaster had my number anyway.

The next day it rang at nine in the morning – it woke me up. Because the room was so small I could reach it by wriggling my belly along the floor a little and stretching, but I left it to ring six or seven times letting it reach each corner of the apartment and settle in. As I picked up the receiver something crashed at the other end and there was a stunning pause so I guessed it was Mr Moriya.

'Hello?' he said at last. 'Hello? Anna san?'

'Hello?'

'Hello! – it's me, Moriya san, are you well? Did you sleep well?'

There was a big firework display in Matsushima that evening as part of the *o-bon* festival for the dead, and Sato sensei had offered to drive us there in his new car with a CD player. Mr Moriya sounded excited, especially about the CD player. He was less coherent than usual over the telephone and I thought this rather endearing – his hopelessness in the face of technical advance. The trouble was, I was aware that he thought so too.

They came to pick me up from my apartment at five, and before we set off we went downstairs to where the landlady lived because there were more papers to sign. She was rather cool about having a foreigner living so near, not at all unfriendly but not too friendly either, as if she wanted to keep me at arm's length and have as little direct contact as possible. She preferred to have Mr Moriya as go-between, even for simple things that I

would rather have kept him out of – like telling me where to put
the rubbish and what day paper could be left out for recycling.
And the date of the big rubbish day once a month. The disposal
of rubbish seemed to worry her most. I think she suspected I
might store it all up in my room.

We drove very fast in the white car, but we did not listen to the
CD player because Sato sensei decided that he wanted to tell us
a story that he had been reading to his grandson. I liked
listening to Sato sensei very much, he was a good story-teller,
but afterwards when I recalled the story it became rather
different, reinvented so that I am not sure now what was his
and what is mine, and what is much, much older. All I
remember is that Oimatsu and Wakamatsu had rather small
roles in Sato sensei's version – in his the Emperor was the
central figure. But even so, Oimatsu and Wakamatsu did the
diving.

There was once a beautiful bay which opened wide into the
Pacific sea, and in its mouth grew hundreds of tiny islands so
that from high above the land looked like a giant whale lying
with its jaws calmly open, awaiting the small creatures drifting
in. Some of the islands did not even reach up through the
water's surface but rested just under it, housing rock crabs and
shallow water fish. Some were large enough to hold a tree or a
patch of coarse grass, some a group of trees with roots knotted
together, wrestling for space, their tops falling outwards over
the sea like a floating *ikebana*.
    On one of the islands in this bay lived a mother and daughter,
named Oimatsu and Wakamatsu. Oimatsu had been in love
with a singer, and he had sung while she had dived for pearls.
He had sung to her underwater, and could tell her when storms
were coming. They lived together in the village by the shore,
and lived comfortably for pearls were precious to the villagers in
those days – they could counter decay and were said to make
the dead immortal. All over the land, underground, pearls
could be found each of which symbolised a risen corpse. And
many of Oimatsu's pearls were placed in the mouths of the
dead.

The singer and Oimatsu had two children, a boy and a girl, but not many years after their birth both father and son became sick and died. Because Oimatsu's diving made her wealthy, several men were eager to marry her, but she rejected them all. However, one morning she was resting on the shore when a rich man, well-respected in the village, came to her and tried to persuade her to be his mistress. He would not listen to her refusals and eventually he grew angry and twisted her to the ground, trying to claim her through raping her. As she screamed, the spirits of the people made immortal through her pearl-fishing rose up out of the land and sea and clung to her attacker, chasing him as a huge cloud of eyes, mouths and hands, through the village and over the hills.

After this Oimatsu took Wakamatsu to live on the islands.

One of the tales that the villagers told, and that Oimatsu would tell her daughter as they sat together on their rock looking out into the Pacific, was the story of the Kusangi sword.

There had been a large battle at sea and the leader of this battle was the boy-Emperor Antoku Tenno. The child could not even lift the familial sword, which had led his ancestors to victory. Instead he played on the sand and the waves placed the wreckage of his army before him. At last his grandmother, knowing that all was lost, crept out one night and threw the sword into the sea, jumping in after it with the sleeping boy in her arms. No one had seen the sword since, but it was thought that it lay somewhere on the sea-bed off this shore.

When Oimatsu was about fifty years old the Emperor Go Shirakawa came to the throne. He was young and much gentler than his predecessor, but neighbouring countries soon heard of his softness and planned to take over his land. The Emperor despised huge military displays and was loath to send any of his subjects to battle if it could be avoided, so he decided to try and trace the Kusangi sword which might enable him to win the battle without killing.

One night in a dream the Emperor was visited by the grandmother of Antoku Tenno and she told him that the sword could be found in the dragon kingdom beneath the sea, not far from Matsushima.

The Emperor set off up north, and heralds travelled ahead to prepare the villagers, for it was as if the sun had decided to visit the earth. On reaching Matsushima, the heralds were told about Oimatsu and Wakamatsu and the mother and daughter agreed to try diving for the sword. They rowed to the outskirts of the bay at dusk. It was windy and the sea reached into the boat, waves somersaulted backwards off the sides of the island rocks, but as the women dived they left the storm on the other side of the water and slipped down through a glassy calm.

Neither had dived so deep before. They passed through a darkness which pressed against them so hard that they could feel the shape of their bodies as the inside of a mould, and feel the throbbing of their blood against the outer shape. As they came down through this darkness it felt as a baby must feel pressed into life – and then all was colour. Plants like sea roses, but turquoise and orange, formed an arch through which the divers swam, and the water was filled with red pearls floating on the currents. They came to the walls of a pearl city, the gate of which was guarded by a ring of dolphins who tightened their loop as the divers tried to enter, leaving no space to swim through. When they explained their mission Oimatsu and Wakamatsu were led through streets cobbled with shells, past houses made of hollowed coral, from the crevices of which bright eyes peeped.

Their dolphin guide paused before a building of coral inside which the dragon lay with the boy-Emperor asleep in its peacock feather scales and the sword by its side. The dragon told them that the Emperors had been mistaken in thinking that the sword belonged above water. It had been borrowed once, and when it was not returned the dragon had taken the form of a princess, married the Emperor of Japan, and after many years become the grandmother of the boy-Emperor Antoku Tenno. For the dragon could not simply steal the sword.

Oimatsu and Wakamatsu spoke for a long time with the dragon, and succeeded at last in winning its trust, assuring it that the sword would be returned immediately to the sea. Then the dolphins carried the women back through the layers of colour and pressure to the surface.

The sword was used and the battle was won, but the Emperor was reluctant to give back the weapon and in order to keep peace between land and sea the divers had to smuggle it to the water, though sometimes the return is credited to a Korean thief who lost the sword at sea while trying to sail back home.

We drove past a sign telling us that Matsushima was one of the three major sights of natural beauty in Japan, and there was a drawing of a small island sprouting a few pine trees.

Lanterns were hung along the main street and stalls with red banners sold sticks of grilled squid, noodles, chocolate-coated bananas and other festival foods, but we didn't have time to eat because we had to find a place from which to watch the fireworks. Although there were thousands of spectators the atmosphere was very calm, and most people were already seated, on the promenade, the grass, and the beachy banks on either side of the bay. Families sat around boxes filled with rice balls, chicken legs, and hard boiled eggs. Even young couples laid out square cloths to mark their places.

The cloths were placed edge to edge, except for the thin lines left to walk along, neat like rice-fields, like the *kanji* for rice-field which is a grid, a square divided in four. I thought of this as I followed Sato sensei and Moriya sensei, placing foot after foot, apologising when a foot missed the line and touched for a second someone's square.

'We'll have to go right down by the sea,' Moriya sensei called back to me.

A boy was holding onto the edge of his family's square and rearing the side up, pretending that the cloth was alive and rising. He reminded me of a summer when I was eight and stayed with a friend in Devon, and how everything had been sucked into our only two frames for the world then – animals and *The Phoenix and the Carpet*. One day, bored in the centre of Plymouth, we remembered that we had left some of the animals in the car.

'Can we go back to get our animals?' my friend asked her mother.

'Where are they?'

'In the car. In the boot of the car.'

'No,' said her mother. So my friend nudged me.

'Can we go back to get our animals, please, Mrs Elliot?' And I

24

added that I thought they would be getting worried about us, in case that helped.

'We'll be finished soon,' Mrs Elliot had said. Then she had an amazingly good idea. 'Why don't you two go back and fetch them on a magic carpet?'

We didn't know whether to be embarrassed that she knew of our games or pleased that she was one of us after all.

'So, what shall we use as a carpet?' Mrs Elliot asked. We were both eyeing her headscarf, but that was the one thing she could not see, so we gave her time to think of it. There was nothing else we could use.

'How about a jacket?' she asked, and we both shook our heads, without taking our eyes off the scarf. There were colourful swirls all over it. It would be just the thing. And finally she had given in because, she said, we exasperated her.

I was picturing myself and my friend sitting cross-legged on the beautiful scarf in the middle of the Plymouth pavement, with crowds of shoppers passing us by like waves below, when I almost bumped into Mr Moriya because he had stopped.

'We have to fold our cloth in half,' he said. 'This is the biggest space we can find.'

From where we sat we could just see a few of the lanterns lit for the dead ancestors floating off across the bay, tipping a little. Now and then one disappeared altogether, for once the candle got wet we could not see its continuing through the darkness. Just before the fireworks started it seemed that there was silence over the bay and among the seated crowds, and then a white plume cut the sky in half with a sound like silk slitting and the darkness became full of star fragments, suspended, then falling, falling into the sea.

On my first morning in school Moriya sensei and I went to meet the Headmaster. We were all bowing and *yoroshiku*-ing for so long that Moriya sensei forgot whose room he was in and said very grandly, 'Please, sit down.' The Headmaster blushed and looked confused, and just stood there in silence while Moriya sensei held out his hands towards the large leather armchairs. Then he must have looked down and seen that they were not his chairs at all, but those of his superior, and he gasped and almost put his hand to his mouth. The Headmaster pretended to laugh it off, though I could see from the start that he was very disdainful. Moriya sensei seemed not to notice this.

The Headmaster looked the absolute opposite of Mr Moriya – comfortable and sedate. He wore a very pale grey suit which fell soft and straight around him, and when he pulled the material slightly above his knees as he sat down the movement was understated, I would not have noticed it at all had Mr Moriya not tugged up his trousers at the same time so that his legs showed white through the gaps above his socks.

'You are from London, England, and you are twenty-two years old, correct?' he asked in English after we had all finally settled and were sipping tea.

'What do you think of Japan?'

I realised, as I was asked this yet again, that I had been missing the point. This talking was not so inane as I had supposed – I was beginning to believe myself when I said 'the scenery is beautiful, the people are friendly'.

The Headmaster spoke to me in English, glancing down at a list of phrases which he had prepared. He said it was an honour to have a speaker of real English in the school.

'King's English,' Moriya sensei interrupted, nodding wisely.

'Queen's, I think,' I smiled a little patronisingly.

Ignoring us, the Headmaster said that he hoped the year

would bring many great times and true opportunities for communication, for that was to be the theme of the next millennium. After this his rhetoric deserted him. He turned over his note and found that there was nothing written on the other side. To fill in the silence, Moriya sensei pointed out that I was 'an academic of English Literature', which received a curt nod as the Headmaster looked down at his watch. Perhaps he felt he had not spent enough time with us, for although he clearly had better things to do than amuse two lunatics, he took a deep breath and began to run through the history of the school's past Headmasters whose severe faces looked down on us, frames tilting slightly forward from the wall. Mr Moriya, stunning us both now by his lack of etiquette, offered me another biscuit. At this, the Headmaster gave up and very politely dismissed us. We bowed out backwards.

The next thing to organise, Mr Moriya told me as we returned to our desks in the so-called academic staffroom, was my stage appearance at the opening assembly.

He pulled an enormous piece of white card from behind his desk and asked me to guess what it was for. I said I had no idea. Some of the teachers at the desks around us were watching with interest and I turned to nod and smile but Mr Moriya had not introduced me formally yet. It was a little like being something he had brought from home. His. When he saw my attention wandering, he said he would introduce me properly to every-one after assembly, but we had a busy hour ahead and he did not want to hurt anyone's feelings by missing them out at this stage. It sounded reasonable.

The card was to make a sign with my name on, which he would hold up as I made my opening speech. He kept talking without pausing at all, except in mid-sentence, and he told me to watch carefully what he did so I was not able to look anywhere but at him. He seemed thirsty for someone to appreciate his calligraphy brush and his top quality ('antique') ink slate with an intricate phoenix-like creature carved along the top like the decoration on a gravestone. He asked me to stroke the black surface of the slate which was soft and cool. Then he wetted it and made it shine, rubbing it with a stub of solid ink until enough thick black liquid appeared to fill his brush. His movements were deliberate and strangely overpowering.

'That's a phoenix carved there, isn't it?' I said, needing to hear my own voice.

'Tell me, what does Anna mean?'

I did know once, but at that moment I could not remember. In the English dictionary on his desk it listed 'Anna' as a quantity of money, originally a Hindu word.

'I didn't know that,' I said. It was not the meaning I thought I knew. Was it something to do with bees? But I sounded unsure. It wasn't much help.

'We can say it is a very old name with roots in nature and in ancient Indian culture. How about it?'

It did not sound very satisfactory, but if it pleased him . . .

'Your surname is easy,' he continued. 'Heron is of course a very gracious bird.'

The card covered both our desks, and it seemed a pity to write on it. Then slowly he formed the first black line, and as he continued he told me how to hold the brush, how to move the wrist exactly so. He said he would be giving me calligraphy lessons soon.

From the stage I felt like I was addressing a very quiet army. A thousand students faced me row after row, the boys in black Prussian military suits, the girls in brown skirts and brown waistcoats. There were hardly any girls at all – perhaps one in ten – most of them in the lines marked 'interior' which meant they were specialising in interior design as opposed to chemistry, electronics, engineering and the other subjects that a technical school offers.

While I read my speech Mr Moriya, dressed in a tail suit, marched up and down with the sign we had made, showing first one side of the hall, then the other, then coming down centre stage. His lips were curved downwards around his chin, and his back was stiff and straight as a Victorian's.

The canteen was empty as I sat down with my bowl of noodles which was all that was being served. I broke the wood chopsticks apart and started to eat. Some students came in and after they had ordered their food two of them came up to me, a brave one who asked questions and a shy one who translated. I thought, this is it, this is what the year will be like. But after asking for my name again, and my country, again, and my town, they said, 'sorry, must go now' and shuffled away giggling. Their friends cheered, patting their backs as they sat down on the benches to eat, and one or two glanced over their shoulder at me with cool curiosity.

A teacher came in and I caught his eye in the hope that he might come and sit by me, but he nodded stonily and went to the opposite corner of the room.

So I ate quickly, slurping, and left, throwing my chopsticks into a huge bucket because these ones were not re-used despite the campaigns run by some of the foreign teachers in the prefecture. I met a woman at the opening conference who had the crazed puritanical look of a missionary, only her mission was to get the Japanese to use less wood. She would speak about it with such passion that she got all us new teachers vowing to change our school canteens from disposable to washable the week we arrived, but I didn't feel I had the energy right now.

As I was leaving, Mr Moriya came up and told me he had had an idea. I thought it a bit odd that he couldn't leave me alone for twenty minutes and yet abandoned me just when I needed him back in the canteen. But when he told me that from now on he would ask his wife to make a packed lunch for me every day, as she made his, I felt bad that I had misjudged him, and accepted readily.

Moriya sensei's desk was on my right and on my left sat Ishikawa sensei. He was about thirty-five, the youngest of the three English teachers, and he didn't talk much, but on the day we planned our first class together he was extremely keen to teach the students a song from *The Sound of Music*.

'Isn't it a good idea?' he asked me with enthusiasm.

He was full of good ideas. He had just been on a weekend course for English teachers and had returned with a book of notes on teaching Conversational Style.

'Some teachers speak rather poorly, so it is a great problem to teach this style.'

'That's what I'm here for,' I said, trying to be jolly, immediately regretting my blunder as he blushed.

'My English is no good,' he shook his head.

'I didn't mean that at all – your English is brilliant. Your accent is perfect.' I hoped these compliments sufficed.

'No, no,' he sighed. 'You are too kind.' Perhaps I should have continued to protest, for after a brief pause he continued, 'But I do practise every day, with the radio, you know.'

We planned how to teach 'These are a few of my favourite things'. At the conference, he had been told to use picture cards.

'For sixteen-year-olds?' I couldn't help asking, and he nodded in reply, quite oblivious to my scepticism.

So we sat down to draw pictures. Girls in white dresses with blue sashes. Raindrops on eyelashes. Brown paper packages. Kittens.

Mr Moriya watched us out of the corner of his eye, and I watched him out of the corner of mine – he did not turn any pages.

Ishikawa sensei hummed the tune to himself as he coloured in a kitten with his felt tip pen.

'I remember the first time I ever saw it,' he said dreamily. 'It was the week that I met my wife.'

'I didn't see it till I was about sixteen,' I told him. 'I used to enjoy saying that I hadn't seen it when everyone else had seen it twenty times, but then one day I watched a bit of it by mistake, and then I thought I might as well sit through the whole thing.' We were very relaxed, side by side, sharing the felt tips.

'What else do we need?' I asked. 'Teddy bears? Strawberries?' I couldn't remember the words so he sang out loud for me. Moriya sensei actually looked up and put on his glasses.

'I'll be having lunch soon,' he said down his nose. 'If you can spare Anna sensei for a few moments.'

'I'm sorry, of course, of course.' Ishikawa sensei made a little bow. 'We'll continue after lunch if that is possible?'

'By all means,' my supervisor replied, with a generous wave of his hand.

The class was the last lesson of the day, and the students, all boys, were waiting to go off to their clubs. Some had already changed into baseball costumes although this was not allowed. Ishikawa sensei reminded them, humbly, and one or two of the boys shuffled a bit, while others gazed out of the window.

He asked if anyone knew *The Sound of Music*. At the English conference a lot had been said concerning the new theory of asking questions which do not have right or wrong answers.

'That's the good thing about this school,' Ishikawa sensei said to me in the silence when nobody answered. 'In academic schools we cannot try new methods because pupils still have to take the old-fashioned university exams. These students know they will not be able to go to university.' I shifted uncomfortably, wanting to remind him he was in front of a class.

After a time Ishikawa sensei tried an older tactic, which did not suit him at all.

'Toyota!' he shouted. 'Have you seen *The Sound of Music*?' The boy stood up and sat down again abruptly, then pointed to his nose and looked to his right and left to see if it was really him being picked on. He pointed at his nose again and Ishikawa sensei nodded patiently.

It was a common response this, and never failed to amuse

foreigners – the look of panic at being singled out. But when I saw this boy I felt he was not really scared, just performing a small day-to-day ritual, separating himself from the class for a moment as unconsciously as a passer-by bows on entering a group. He stood up again.

'I don't know,' he said, and everyone laughed.

'What do you mean? Do you understand the question?'

'I don't know.'

'Have you ever seen *The Sound of Music*? – the film – *The Sound of Music*?'

'I don't know.'

'Okay, sit down.' The boy sat, and immediately began giggling with a friend. Ishikawa sensei asked the class again. There was a pause, then a boy at the back raised his fist with a shout as though he had scored a goal.

'Yes!'

Everyone laughed again, for this was the class joker.

'Good,' Ishikawa sensei smiled innocently. 'Now we are going to learn a song from it. Anna sensei and I have drawn cards for you to make it easier.' They went quiet, but I suspected less than half of them were even attempting to listen. However, they were alert enough to leap up when the tape recorder came on, and while some did not even mouth the words, one or two of them sang very well, and others – the group of wilder students who always hovered at the back – appeared to enjoy the silliness and made the room shake with their performance.

Ishikawa sensei seemed pleased with the way the lesson had gone.

'At least I put some theory into practice,' he said, as we walked back to the staffroom.

At the end of my first week a welcome party was given by all the English teachers and we went to a restaurant in the part of town where most of the big offices were, up near the prefectural office. We all went together in Sato sensei's car and, as it was the first time Ishikawa sensei had been in it, he spent most of the journey complimenting Sato sensei on the seats, the electronic seatbelts, the smooth movement of the sunroof as it peeled back in silence. Ishikawa sensei was saving up for a portable computer.

'He is a lucky man,' said Sato sensei to me. 'He has no children, so he can buy such things when he is still young.' Almost the first thing Ishikawa sensei had said to me was that he had no children, that he had a Persian cat instead, that it was something to do with his wife, so I felt embarrassed – but Ishikawa sensei did not seem to mind.

There was a lot of traffic on the roads and it would have been quicker to walk.

'Will you be able to drink?' I asked Sato sensei, knowing that the drinking and driving laws were very strict, and wanting something to say. He laughed. His sense of humour always puzzled me, but I liked him. His eyes were high up like a frog's and this apparently made him an expert mushroom picker (I hadn't cracked this joke yet, and had begun to suspect that despite the tearful laughter nobody else had either).

'I do not drive back home tonight, it is okay.'

'So where will you stay?' For a moment I thought maybe we were all expected to stay up through the night, partying. They all laughed at me then.

'Do you not have drive-home-service in London? Someone drives you home in your car, and another car follows behind to pick the driver up afterwards, like a driver and taxi service in one.'

'A *chauffeur*,' said Mr Moriya. 'They use the French term in England.'

I had gone into school early that day as I was teaching first lesson and, although there was another hour until the students arrived, many of the staff were already in, one or two asleep as if they had been hunched over their desks all night. Not that anyone was working, that was not the point. I had entered the school gates, a car drew up alongside me, driven by a woman in her mid-fifties with hair scooped back in a tight bun, and on the reclining seat next to her lay one of the maths teachers, asleep with his mouth open. At first I thought I should offer to help her carry him in, but as I watched she leant across his chest to open the door and then nudged him hard with her elbow so that he nearly rolled straight out. He grunted and began to get up – before he had even closed the door the woman drove off, slamming it shut as she went up the road. Neither of them had exchanged a word.

Laid out on the low table on white rectangular plates with legs were four enormous clams – twice, even three times as big as my fist and knobbled and irregular. Mine had some barnacles on it as well. The bottom and top halves were separated by a finger-thick crack reaching from side to side and curving up very slightly like a grin. An old squat face. All I could think of to say was how old it must have been. How long it must have waited deep down in the sea, watching the fish go by, watching the nets trailing, growing in peace, patient, allowing the odd barnacle to nestle in its crevices. It was ridiculous. I didn't want to eat it.

We poured each other beer and each of us gave a brief speech promising to make the most of our year together.

'Cheers,' Mr Moriya and I said together and we leant across our clams and clinked glasses. '*Kampai*.' The others did the same, touching my glass, then his glass.

'Now the Great Englishman is satisfied,' laughed Sato sensei, which seemed an odd remark but I was busy looking at the barnacles out of the bottom of my eye.

Delicately, I opened my shell, watching how the others pulled theirs apart. The centre, the creature, looked familiar and then I realised it was like the liperma lump of fat that I had had taken out of my back when I was eighteen. The doctor had showed it to me afterwards, and it was white with fine pinkish veins.

'I don't think I can eat this,' I said feebly, my throat gagging in preparation.

'It does not taste,' said Sato sensei, who had already eaten his. 'Just salt.'

Ishikawa sensei held his piece between his chopsticks and nibbled a corner before putting the rest in his mouth. Mr Moriya ate his in one go, then took a gulp of *sake*, and I thought that looked a good strategy. They were all watching me. It seemed impossible to refuse. Then Mr Moriya said, 'Of course you don't have to eat it,' and there was a strange glimmer in his eye, which made me look away from him rather too abruptly. I picked up the creature and put it in my mouth, which it filled snugly. The salt taste shot up my tongue and I swallowed. As it went down through me I felt it was cleaning me, it was like taking a capsule of sea air. I could feel it settle low in my stomach.

'If you grow them on farms,' Mr Moriya said, 'the shapes are not so interesting. It is quite a fine distinction, a matter of taste.'

'I wonder if they re-use the shells then,' I said, but both he and Sato sensei threw their heads back and roared with laughter as if I had made a very funny joke. The clam was heavy and cool inside me, right at the centre, as if I was now its shell and we were still happy in the sea – or something. The beer and *sake* were already swirling inside us all.

In retrospect we talked very little that evening, but drank and laughed and remarked on how delicious each course was. There were twenty dishes in all, though some were almost entirely decorative, a slice of aubergine with a chrysanthemum served on a leaf, and a little pot of chicken pieces served in soft scrambled egg which is called, familiarly, Mother and Child.

All the meal through I could sense the clam in me, making me very calm, but not wholly dispelling the loneliness.

Back to the Moriya household again. At midday, the day after the English party, Saturday, I was still in bed.

It would be nice, I thought, watching the sunlight through my curtains, to spend the weekend alone. Or if not alone, with someone I haven't been sitting next to all week. But it didn't seem like there was much choice. I had said I would be at their house by lunch-time. Already I was leaving my futon unfolded some days, even though it made me depressed when I came back in and couldn't see the floor.

I had forgotten the number of the bus so I walked all the way from the subway station terminal. Looking around, it was like I imagined America would be, the roads wide and lined with drive-in Mcdonald's, Wild West cafés and huge video rental stores. And there were the pachinko halls which hummed perpetually with the clink and splatter of a thousand metal pellets falling and hitting and missing each other. Between all these buildings there were a few small rice-fields still, and in one of them an old woman was bending down, picking up litter – hamburger boxes and vivid blue pocari sweat cans.

There were some wild flowers in the scrubland in front of the Moriyas' house, and they had begun to build an arched wooden gateway to mark the beginning of their garden now that almost all the land had been sold. The windows were open so I could look straight in on the corridor, and through to the main *tatami* room, the 'guest room', the paper doors of which were drawn back. Mr Moriya sat cross-legged at the low table, laying out paper, brushes, slate and blocks of black ink.

'Hello!' he called, rising to come to the doorway. 'You are just on time, everything is ready for a calligraphy class, how about it?'

Mrs Moriya took my bag and before I realised what she was

36

doing she had carried it to her daughter's room. I followed Mr Moriya, as bidden, into the guest room and knelt at the table. We seemed to be missing out lunch – I wondered if they had eaten already – but when Mrs Moriya returned she told him that we had better eat first.

His hands travelled across the paper so slowly I could hardly see them move. Slowly a dark dot became a little longer, a little longer, and then finally a flick upwards, a spiked tail, and that one was over. Again he dipped the brush in and touched the paper and dragged the brush and again and again until a corner of the paper was filled. Then he moved on a fraction into a clean space. I slouched further into the cushion, letting my feet stick out sideways.

A bird came and stood in the corridor with its head on one side, watching us. It hopped along the wood a little, but then skidded on the shiny surface and flew off.

'Pass the water,' he said, and I passed it again. He dropped two drops onto the slate. The squeak and grate as he rubbed the block of ink against the smooth surface, round and round, up and down, creating the thick black paint, had begun to pester me, its echo vibrating just under my skin, sending shivers up my back. I itched too, I touched one itch and another started. I tried to find the cool clam in me to see if it would calm me again, but I could not feel it there anymore.

'Watch carefully,' he said, and then at last,

'What have I written?' He knows quite well I cannot read.

'I don't know.'

'This,' he said, 'is my name, and this is today's date, and this is a verse of a poem about the moon over Matsushima. See, here are the *kanji* for Matsushima, see, you recognise it?'

'Oh yes,' I said, rather than be taught that once more.

'Now, you have a go, how about it?'

Relieved to be moving I knelt upright again – reached for the water – watched it darken and thicken with satisfaction.

'That's very good. Your wrist movement is very good.'

I chose a brush (Ah, you have good taste, good taste) and let it drink in the blackness. Then I touched the paper and made a beautiful black dot, and kept my brush there. I couldn't think what to write. I didn't want to do any of the really easy *kanji* like mountain, river or person, and I couldn't think of any others. The dot was getting too big – it was going to ruin whatever I attempted now.

'Careful,' breathed Mr Moriya. 'It is smudging.'

'I'm trying to remember the *kanji* for England,' I said through clenched teeth, and as I spoke I could feel my hand forming, mouthing the strokes although it was still. And then slowly it began to move along in a line. I raised the brush to add the two little strokes which pierced the first line vertically through.

'Good.'

In my mind I threw the brush down, ripped the paper in two. I went faster. I wanted to rush – to run. And then I was enjoying it, it seemed wonderful to me that without actually being able to picture the interlocking lines as a whole, the character flowed from my hand perfectly once I had learnt its rhythm. As easy as writing in English. Better done fiercely. I flushed with pleasure as I replaced the brush.

'You started well, but from here it is not so good. Try again.'

I ground the ink harder still, but felt nothing of the beauty now, as the brush sucked up the blackness. The ink clogged and would not flow. I tried to soften my fingers, and the line I was on wobbled and swerved. It looked even worse this time.

'Try again.' I shouted *no!* but no sound came out. The blood was pounding in my head and I could not think of any way to get away except by shouting *no*. And I was a guest, how could I say it?

'Try again.'

On the fourth attempt he said perhaps I should try with 'day' or with 'rice-field' or with 'river'.

I tried 'rice-field', but although it was simple, because it was simple, it looked clumsy.

He took the brush from me. His hands were enormous.

'Watch.'

But now I could not tell what made it good or bad. I thought his rice-field looked clumsy too, but he seemed to think it was beautiful.

'By the end of the year you will do it like this,' he smiled – he actually smiled – as if he had really noticed nothing. 'Try again.'

'Try again.'

'Perhaps Anna sensei is tired,' I heard Mrs Moriya's voice over my shoulder, and fell off my cushion with relief.

'Anna sensei!'

I looked up and a young man whom I did not know was smiling down at me.

'I am a *Sannensei* – Third Year – student at the Technical High. I know you.'

I was sunbathing on my stomach, but as I knelt up I folded the towel across my knees, self-consciously.

'My name is Suzuki Kazuo. I want to learn English from you but you are not teaching in my homeroom. I am sorry.' He frowned sweetly.

'Nice to meet you, Kazuo.' I shielded my eyes and held out a wet hand.

And then he was gone.

The pool sides were emptying now, and children were being dressed. Beside me a man leapt about on the edge of the floppy diving board. He had been up and down the plank all day, but all he would do was bounce in a fancy way, and then when he thought no one was looking he would stroll back along the way he had come, whistling. He must have been terrified of the water, and yet like a silly moth he came back and back to play with the idea of entering it.

I too must have looked silly as I swam luxuriously in the suddenly emptied pool, before noticing the poor guard pulling at his hair, too nervous to tell me that it was 'rest time' and that we had all been ordered out of the water.

I wondered if Kazuo had seen this.

I liked his face enormously, and his smile lingered for a while after he had left.

'You remember I said I was only wanting a graduate of English literature?'

We had just taught our second class together – with the text book – a story about a little girl who looked after her crippled mother patiently all through the war and then died of tuberculosis at its very end. When her body was found she was clutching a rice ball which people said she must have been saving for her little brother. So a statue was built to commemorate her goodness, and now school-children visited it to pay homage to her. No one else seemed to think it was funny.

Now we entered the staffroom together and, although all the other teachers who were free sat in the smoking corner and played cards, we strode directly to our desks.

'I wanted someone with knowledge of old-style English because I need help with something.'

I listened as I put my papers away.

'You see, remember I told you that I was a scholar at heart?' I remembered him saying he was Romantic, I did not think I had heard the scholarly bit, but I nodded.

'Please, look at this,' he offered me a small white book, watching my face for any change in my eyes as I read the *kanji* for his name on the cover.

'You can read it?' he asked, pleading with me.

'By you?'

'It's a top publisher. Look inside.'

It was a book of English epitaphs, with translations in Japanese, for he was a translator of gravestones. Inside the front cover he had written in careful calligraphy with sharply poised edges, 'To my dear Anna sensei, in expectation of long and beautiful friendship.'

'For you,' he beamed. 'This is my work of art, my scholarship. I am the only translator of epitaphs in Japan. I am quite famous

41

in this field.' His hands were crossed, resting on his knees.

> Alack and well-a-day
> Potter himself has turned to clay.

'This is the top academic publisher in this country.'
'Thank you,' I said.

> Here lies the Mother of children five
> Three daughters dead two sons alive.
> The daughters died because they'd rather
> Go to their Mother than stay with their Father.

'I think it is a pity we do not have such a tradition in Japan.'
He asked me to help him sometimes with his work, said he had some queries, that it would be 'a pleasant pass time' for us. I flicked through the pages, distracted, trying to distance myself from him and the part he wanted me to play. I said that I would help him if ever I had time, but as I spoke my voice got harder and my eyes were telling him to leave me alone. My heart was pounding again.
'Thank you. I'll enjoy looking at it,' I said, putting the book in my bag.

While I marked papers, I felt him next to me. I did not feel Ishikawa sensei who sat on the other side. Even when he was restrained, when he sat like now, his head bowed, his knees neatly together, his expensive English shoes snapped into a pair – even now he seemed physically loose. His mouth was dropping down at the corners and his face was moist, his hands fiddled with his fountain pen.

I tried to ignore him and in my efforts to draw other pictures forth, I came across a worse thing. On television the night before there had been a close-up of a woman's face. She looked bruised, bloated and it caught my eye so I turned to watch. The camera panned out, and she was hanging from a tree. As it panned further you could see detectives all around her, in and out of the bushes, gathering evidence, and she just hung in a blue skimpy dress in the middle of them.

They didn't cut her rope. *Why don't they cut the bloody rope?*

I tried to replace her with the calm-faced angel on the cover of the gravestone book, but that didn't work, so I surrendered.

'I'll look through some of the translation queries now if you want.' He stood up, put on his glasses and pressed them into the bridge of his nose, which always made him wince. And he fumbled with thick fingers through the shelves above his desk for the notebook which he was storing questions in. On the front it read 'Questions for Anna sensei' in swirly writing.

He sat back and folded his hands primly, watching me.

A little later, a student came in to say hello to me. In a strong American accent learned from *Sesame Street*, she asked me to start up an English Speaking Society because that was what a foreign teacher in her friend's school had done. She teased Mr Moriya about his preference for England over the United States, saying it was a poor unvaried little island, as bad as Japan. I wondered why I could not tease him like that.

Her name was Miyo and she was in love with Arnold Schwarzenegger, she said.

Above The Perfect Bathroom Store on Ichibancho there was a restaurant which specialised in potatoes. It was called something like Sami's Spuds and all the dishes were based on potatoes – potatoes cooked in more or less any way that you wanted, with cheese, with seaweed, in fish cakes.

One afternoon I was in Maruzen trying to decide whether to buy *The Gods Will Have Blood* at great expense (not only to read – I wanted a copy of the painting by Marat on the cover) when James came up to me.

'How's it going?' he asked.

'I'm just thinking of buying a book.'

'Looks violent,' he grinned, glancing down.

'A woman did it,' I muttered.

'Excuse me? Oh, it's written by a *woman* is it?' he said wittily.

'No, a woman killed him.'

He had an hour to kill himself, he said. Would I go to Sami's Spuds with him? Had I been? And as I was feeling hungry and in need of some English conversation I agreed to go.

Being above the shops on Ichibancho the customers were almost all women. We discussed very briefly and without much enthusiasm why Japanese men seemed more conservative in their eating habits than Japanese women. I recounted some anecdote about a teacher in my school who had recently been to China and said he refused to eat the rice there because it was such bad quality. James had an identical story about noodles.

I said that the buttered potato cakes on the table next to us looked good but James felt like a full meal. I wondered whether I should show him the way to fold a tea ceremony cloth with my paper napkin, but decided against it.

A waiter welcomed us and brought the menu, which was covered in dancing potato people. One potato was wearing a ballet costume and smiled blandly. James said that he'd have that one, please, but the waiter did not understand.

We ordered set meals and James, who had been living in the city for over a year and felt it his duty to explain things, told me how the *setu* was simply a neat way to market a variety of different dishes while appearing to maintain the old custom which required everyone to order the same as their neighbour.

'It takes a bit of getting used to, this country,' he said, trying to be kind because he thought I'd gone too quiet. 'You'd never guess it, but I think I'm going to be marrying here.'

I looked up at his clean rosy face.

'The trouble is, she was one of my students last year.'

'Oh.' Maybe he hoped for an argument.

'I know it doesn't look too good, but it's not what it sounds. I didn't even teach her. She was in the final year and she's left now. I thought you might be angry,' he added, as I remained silent. 'Do you know Christobel? From Australia? She'll be furious with me.'

'Is that what you're hoping?' I asked nastily. But the bitterness seemed to bounce straight off him and back at me.

'So you're a feminist are you?' he grinned. 'And I bet you're against nuclear weapons too.'

'What's that supposed to mean?'

'And I bet your arguments could be broken just –' he picked up a toothpick and snapped it in two '– like that.' He was laughing.

'But I'm not going to let you get anywhere near my arguments,' I smiled. 'I'm English – I'm reserved, remember. And I wish you all the best for the future.'

The first meeting of the English Speaking Society was held informally by the river so that everyone could chat about what they wanted to get out of it. Some of the *Ichinensei* – First Year – girls organised a game – blind somebody's something – a version of What's the time, Mr Wolf? And we played that for a while, in English, until everyone was screaming and laughing and some of the girls had begun to fall onto the three boys who were present. Then we sat down on the concrete river bank to talk.

'We want to learn English to have fun with,' said Kazuo, the boy from the swimming-pool. 'Not for exams, for – for being with people.'

'For communication,' Miyo added.

The river was quite high from the recent rain and the current was fast. We planned to meet once a week and talked about the excursions we would make, the talking we would do, while we watched the rubbish go by, pieces of blue plastic sacking, shreds of cardboard boxes from Australia and South Africa – and endless bottles.

'A dead bird,' said Hiro, the smallest and most silent of the group. He pointed to the centre of the river where the current was passing fastest. Its wings were spread like it was flying still.

'Do you want to have children?' Miyo asked me as we walked back toward the school.

'Some day I'd like to – I'm not in a hurry though – how about you?'

'No *way*,' she laughed. 'And if I did, I'd want to send it to a foreign school, not a Japanese school. But foreign schools are expensive. And I don't want to get married, but if I do not have a husband I cannot pay for a foreign school. That is my problem.'

'A few days ago in the staffroom,' I said, 'two boys from *Ichinensei* were made to kneel on the floor. They were there all morning, kneeling on the floor with books balanced on their heads. I hadn't seen that before. One of the teachers was yelling and yelling at their ears, and when they strained away, he forced their heads back to his lips. And then he spat at them. I hadn't seen that before.'

'Yes, sometimes that happens,' Miyo answered. Her face had hardened and her lips were tight.

It was odd, but I felt gentleness among this group of men in my staffroom. Forty men, desks in rows, and they sat around, sometimes crying with laughter, gossiping, playing card games – not like I imagined forty men in England would be. They placed one foot up on their knee and massaged it while they were chatting. They laid soft hands on each other's shoulders, and giggled like First Year girls.

I saw nothing of any cruelty there might be beneath.

I had tried rice crackers once in England, from a small Japanese shop which had recently opened in Richmond. They were large and not quite crisp after their long journey and when my sister discovered they were not even vegetarian I decided they were not worth pursuing.

Here I couldn't read the ingredients and I had no one to compete with on that score, so it didn't seem to matter very much. And they tasted good. There were more types than I could ever have imagined before I came here and they all had different names like the proverbial Eskimo snow, but I could never remember them. I would say to my students, 'Well, I like the big, nobbled round ones with little bits of seaweed mixed in, rather than stuck on top', and they would try to guess the type. It was a good way of getting them to listen, the kind of game I would do when we had ten minutes at the end of the class and were all sick of hangman.

This particular evening I had a special one, spherical but not perfectly so, and covered with sesame seeds all over so that none of the smooth surface showed at all. I bit it and it had a peanut inside, and the peanut took over the whole flavour so that I couldn't taste the sesame at all. Then there were little rectangles blown up like balloons, with squares of *nori* stuck on haphazardly, as if scattered from quite a distance, or blown on and stuck like autumn leaves. And the speckled red ones, egg shaped, which always had nuts inside. And the spicy crescent shaped ones which I often didn't bother to eat because they stopped me from appreciating the subtlety of the others. And smart ones with a whole small piece of *nori* wrapped round like a neatly tucked bed.

As I was eating my way through these, watching a BBC nature programme and trying to lip-read what the presenter was saying, the telephone rang.

'You know who it is?'

'Yes.'

'It's Mori-chan!' That means, affectionately, 'dear protector'. He asked me to call him that sometimes.

'I know.'

'How about coming to stay again this weekend?'

I had been preparing excuses all through the afternoon classes, expecting him to ask as I left the staffroom – then I had taken the easier option and slipped away through the gates and trotted off along the road when he wasn't looking.

'How about it?'

'I'm not sure.' I twisted the phone cord around my hands till the blood pounded and the flesh was puffy.

'You are not *busy* are you?'

'Well, actually I am rather.'

'What? What are you doing?' There was the glimmer of a razor in his voice – sometimes it frightened me, but tonight with those glorious rice crackers spread out before me, I felt I actually wanted to lie. The possibilities seemed endless.

'I'm meeting an American friend, and I'm going to the cinema, and I might be going to Matsushima on Sunday.'

'Oh,' he said. 'I see. It is a great pity, my wife has prepared some very special dish for you.'

'I'm really sorry.' He sensed the quiver of indecision. 'I didn't know.'

'Could you come for lunch perhaps?'

'Its lunch I'm meeting – the person for.'

He ummed and ahed and I put a sheet of paper between my lips to make sure I kept silent. I couldn't exactly hang up, but the idea was so tempting that I began grinning the paper into a smile, watching myself in the mirror.

At last he gave up.

Immediately I felt sick with guilt – my head a volcano splitting, pouring thick hot lava down my sides – and when the flushing heat subsided I lay down, charred and wretched. The weekend was empty now. The last person I wanted to see was this loon-faced dumb man from the BBC describing exotic animals as if, just by showing us a snatch here and there of their

49

lives, he could tell us what a wonderful, varied place the world was.

I did not understand him.

'What do you want to be?' he asked.
    'I don't know.'
'You could be a professor of English at a women's university. There is a very good one in Tokyo.'
'What do you mean? Why a women's university? Why not a mixed one?'
He chuckled, daddy dinosaur to baby dinosaur.
'I know what you are saying but the atmosphere of a women's university might suit you better, I think. More "seemly" as you say in England.'
'I could teach at Todai.'
'Well . . .'
'But I don't want to teach at all.'
A pause.
'But you want to write books don't you?'
'I don't know,' I repeated, defensive.
'You could write about me.'
I looked up at him and gave him a small, shocked smile.
'Oh no, no. Anyway, I'd never get round to it.' And yet I knew deep down that that was what I planned to do – years from now perhaps – when I would no longer see it as a betrayal. But did he not desire it above everything, a long epitaph – witty and sad?

Yoshimoto sensei was the only other woman who taught in the school, and she rarely came into our staffroom because her desk was in another building. She was the Home Economics teacher. As Moriya sensei said, not academic staff.

I was introduced to her on my first day, and she said at once that it would be nice if I came to stay with her family one weekend. She had a daughter and a son of my age and I would have very much liked to go, but was still awaiting the invitation. She didn't speak any English at all and chatted away to me in Japanese whether I understood or not. I liked that. But most of the time she was busy and I never knew when I could interrupt her. So in general I didn't.

One day though, she invited me to join in with a cookery class – to make lunch with the *Sannensei*, the Final Year students. All girls. Home Economics was compulsory for girls, and rather than abolishing the course there was talk of making it compulsory for boys also. Yoshimoto sensei was looking forward to that.

Her large kitchen was lined with posters of life-saving kisses and lessons in dental hygiene. Along the windowsill, lit now by the sun, stood a series of plastic models which gave a life-size monthly view into a pregnant womb – in the last model, I was told, the baby could be actually pressed out. Compared to more academic schools ours was quite short of money, but Yoshimoto sensei fought to get these models despite reluctance from above.

'It's well worth the money,' she told me with a grin. 'Anything to put these girls off.'

Perhaps her recipes were designed with a similar theme in mind – today certainly the raw materials looked grotesque – but none of the students seemed to mind cutting out fish eyes to use as a decoration round the potato croquettes or massaging the flesh to make the backbone loose so that it would come out whole. They were even having fun pulling the innards out of chickens. A baby rabbit on television, or Chibi Maruko chan, might have been sweet and *kawai*, but not the little dead creatures here.

The soup they were making fascinated me. It was full of tiny fishes – each no longer than my fingernail but made top-heavy by their huge bulging eyes. When I stirred the liquid in my bowl they floated around as if they were alive before slowly settling back down on the bottom with the heavier types of seaweed. It was a bit like a little fish tank, and I couldn't help saying so because I knew it would make them laugh, and it did. Then they enjoyed trying to make me eat *nato* which was a sort of rotten tasting sticky bean mixture – supposed to make foreigners turn away as vampires do from garlic.

When I told the *Ichinensei* students during my very first lesson that they could ask me any questions they liked, three of them had wanted to know whether I could eat *nato*. That was what they wanted to find out above everything else. After the third time I had written it up on the blackboard. NO I CANNOT EAT NATO!

And I had asked them if they could eat lice, and one or two of the braver ones – mishearing me – shouted 'yes!'

In fact I had avoided eating *nato* until now.

Being in a room with forty women made me realise how much I was missing. I felt I could float up to the ceiling, I was so light.

'Always remember that the most important thing is variety,' Yoshimoto sensei told us. 'You should eat at least thirty different types of food each day, in as many textures and colours as possible. This is the best way of ensuring a balanced diet.'

I sat only half-listening, not wanting to return to an afternoon at work on gravestones. There had been talk recently of the school being rebuilt, although this had been promised before. The atmosphere would be quite different without these sad grey walls. From the window, across the brown-grey earth of the playing fields, I could see a shed, which I had been told was the only part of the school to survive from before the war. It was very simple, wood with a small window and a narrow door, slightly raised from the ground. The roof was only corrugated iron, probably not original, but it rather suited it. It was a sad, dignified little building. I hoped they wouldn't knock it down.

After helping with the washing-up I returned to my desk, and only when I saw Mr Moriya hunched over his book and my lunch-box waiting for me, unopened, did I remember that I had forgotten to say where I was going.

I imagined him placing my lunch-box deliberately in the centre of my desk, opening his own *bento*, starting to eat in icy silence.

'I am so sorry,' I pleaded, sitting down beside him.

'Yoshimoto sensei told me,' he said in a decidedly unfriendly voice. 'In fact she told me yesterday that she was going to invite you.' In other words, she had asked permission.

Then why, I thought, have you given me a lunch-box all the same? Why so precisely in the centre of my desk, making me feel guilt as sharp as the point of a knife?

Don't let this happen, I think. Don't let him do this.

'I tasted *nato* for the first time. And I didn't like it much.' I did not know if my hesitancy was acted or real, I had played it to be polite, copying tones I had heard women use, and now all distinction was blurred. I was speaking my English as if it were Japanese, an in-between language of my own. False.

'No foreigners do,' he replied, without looking up from his book.

Autumn

Each year there was a *bunkansai*, a school festival. The students dressed up and paraded through the city centre, from the prefectural office to the school, and the brass band at the front was heralded by Moriya sensei waving his bagpipes, dressed in kilt and Scottish bonnet. This year he wanted to go one better and march arm in arm with an English Farmer's Wife. I guessed who that might be.

'But I don't have a costume – I don't have anything remotely suitable – I don't even know what you mean by English Farmer's Wife,' I said, a little petulant.

'A Farm-girl, you know. My wife has a long and very exquisite lace apron which I gave her as a souvenir from Norwich – how about it?'

During the afternoons preceding the festival, tea ceremony lessons were held for all those who wanted to perform to parents and friends. The tea teacher wore an old blue and white *kimono* made of heavy silk. She had grey hair held in a blue clip and she moved in a slow dance across the *tatami* mats, weaving feet, hands, turning her neck and her waist. She ran her fingers down the thick red silk of the tea ceremony cloth, and her grace and her calmness passed into the material and made it come alive. She wiped the bowl with circular movements, her elbow raised, her underarm forming an arc of strength and delicacy.

I was reminded of the tight shoulders of a Victorian woman in some painting, her arms held to her sides as she poured the tea, restrained, tense, with a frown turning her face prematurely old, for all her energy and her pain was gathering there. Not so our tea teacher, who poured her boiling water onto the green powder with the mesmeric restraint of a magician.

'Wake up, foreign teacher!' Kazuo called through the window, shocking us back to the straining in our bent knees –

shocking everyone by his familiarity with me.

'Could I go home for a bit and sort out a costume?' I suggested, hoping to get out into the sun.

Two months of looking for excuses to leave the school during the day, and the feeling of relief as I left the gates had lost none of its power. The school buildings lifted from my shoulders and spiralled away. Walking softly, slowly, along the hedge, round the corner, elongating the hour.

The large rubbish pile was still there.

On the large rubbish pile at seven that morning there was a child's bicycle, a washing machine, two boxes of pornographic comics, a small electric oven – I took a bookcase and a double futon. By this time all the best things had gone. The second hand appliances shop had turned up as I left for school and taken almost everything, including the comics.

Sorting through my clothes for a peasant outfit or similar, I was aware that the bookshelf had fitted in well and the futon had not. The books looked comfortable, the wood seemed to keep to itself. But the futon made me feel itchy. Pink, with a small stain in one corner. It didn't smell, but it radiated pollution. In one morning it had changed the atmosphere. My eyes kept flicking back to it.

I heard the big rubbish truck arrive and then move on. So either I could play the foreigner and leave it out on the street until next month's collection, or I would have to get used to living with it.

I took it down to the street below.

Dressed in a long skirt, a floppy hat, with a piece of flowery material draped round me and heavy shoes, I looked just about eccentric enough to pass as an English Farmer's Wife. So after an hour I went back to school, smiling to the futon as I passed, and declared that I would need the apron and a wicker basket.

Everyone was pleased with my tea ceremony practice and it helped me get closer to people. I served tea to the gardener with the beautiful face like an ancient giant turtle. He always watched us through the window of the shed and so one day I asked the teacher if I could invite him in. I understood very little of what he said, just his actions and the movements of his eyes.

His wife was Korean apparently. Mr Moriya laughed when I asked what his name was. He spent most of the day watching television in the groundsmen's hut.

Yoshimoto sensei came up to me after a particularly long and painful practice, and massaged my shoulders so that I felt like leaning my head against her and crying with relief.

And then came the festival.

We had a very early start, the students running round the games pitch shouting encouragement to each other. Then there was silence as the final preparations were made.

I went home to dress. At the last minute I wrapped up the bear that I had brought with me – an old bear that had watched over my entire life – I wrapped it up as a baby. Then I put flowers in my wicker basket, glanced at the mirror, and locked my room.

The bear went down very well. It made people overlook my costume, having a baby bear under my arm and me supposed to be a teacher. People were queuing to take photographs.

All the floats and the fancy dressers gathered by the prefectural office. I realised that I was suddenly extremely happy, standing at the town centre amidst crowds of singing teenagers, wearing a long skirt, a shawl, an apron, with a teddy bear held tight under one arm. In the sun.

Moriya sensei turned up with his bagpipes, hat and dish-cloth kilt. He was so flustered that he could not keep hold of me, and I floated around trying to chat informally with some of my students while they put the finishing details to spaceships and dinosaurs.

There was something else I was thinking of. I expected to see Kazuo here, I wanted him to see me dressed up like this, and his presence usually distracted me from Mr Moriya. But he did not come and the parade began.

I walked on the left in front of the trombone. Moriya sensei walked more or less steadily on the right although he swung over towards me to offer various witticisms now and then.

'Ha, ha, English farmer!'

'Teddy bear, very funny!'

Or,

'Would you care to try your hand at the bagpipes?'

At first I stepped up on to the kerb, I looked the other way, and laughed too piercingly with the puzzled trombone player. Then I gave in because it took so much energy to be deliberately unkind. And I could reason, on and off, that he did not deserve such negative attention.

When he asked if I was happy, I turned to him and looked straight into his flushed face.

'Yes.'

Judging the boys dressed as girls competition in the hall later that afternoon, really I was.

Kazuo came to take tea from me wearing the girls' school uniform. He sat on the bench under the red umbrella in the makeshift tea garden – the tea room was only a practice one, too small to perform in, and there was no other *tatami* mat room.

He turned the tea cup three times, perfectly, and handed it back to me with his head bowed very slightly and his mouth curled up at the edges. After I had changed from my *kimono* we set off back towards my apartment together, and he told me that he had never had tea in that way before.

He had followed the diagrams posted above my head.

'I don't really like that kind of thing, but it seemed different taking it from you, informal.'

'I'm very flattered.' But he didn't appear to understand.

The pink futon was still there on the street, luminous in the dusk.

I didn't say it was mine but after he left me at the bottom of the steps leading up to my apartment, I dragged it back up and tried to hide it under papers and suitcases in my cupboard. Although it made me itch to look at it, I learnt to live with it hidden. I missed every big rubbish day, and it ended up sitting out the year with me.

Usually a big drinking party for all the staff was held on the night of the *bunkansai*, but all the sports teachers had to attend a Prefectural Sports Meeting that evening so the party was postponed until two days later. A weekend passed in-between and a sadly normal Monday in school, through which most of us slept.

Lessons finished and few students stayed around for their clubs that afternoon, so the courtyards were unusually silent. Although there was no work to do, the teachers showed no signs of going home. Some were snoring, bent over their desks, and some were chatting and playing *go* in the smokers' corner. Mr Moriya was translating epitaphs, searching for Latin words in his dictionary. There was a list of queries for me to work through placed hopefully in the centre of my desk, and as I hovered, wondering how I might escape, he reached for his spectacles and turned to me.

'Is it clear? My writing is really very poor. Let me go through them with you.'

'It's perfectly clear, really, it's fine.'

But he took the list, holding it in both hands, and began to read through each question elongating every word into something unrecognisable, his mouth forming huge circles which fell round me like a spell and kept me there for the rest of the afternoon, attempting to translate the voices of the dead.

After speeches there was singing and I danced with the Headmaster, formally, stiff as two marble pillars which touch only through an arch. When he had had enough, he bowed to me, with his arm behind his back, and returned to his table. The deputy headmaster patted his shoulder and poured him a beer. No one attempted to approach me, and I turned one way then another, feeling clumsy and lost – the only foreigner, the only woman (Yoshimoto sensei had not come), and easily the youngest.

Hayasaka sensei was laughing with a group of teachers whom I recognised but did not know, and I went up to them tentatively.

'Good dancing,' Hayasaka sensei greeted me. 'How about a dance with me?' He wiggled his hips in a dignified way. 'Come and talk with us.'

He introduced a young man from the electrical department – Sasaki sensei.

'He speaks English very good, much better than me,' he said, but the young man simply said 'Nice to meet you,' and then remained smiling politely. The older teachers appeared to be teasing him, and he drew further back as they pushed him forward.

'Did you like the meal?' someone asked.

'Yes, it was delicious. Especially the tempura, I always like tempura best. And the tofu was very good.'

'Did you like the sashimi?' said another, again in Japanese, rather as if he had been dared to ask me a question.

'Yes, I liked that too,' I said, perhaps rather less enthusiastically, having discovered that it was best to be honest on this front. There was a slight pause, then the questioner coughed delicately and continued,

'This restaurant is famous for its sashimi. It is the best sashimi in Sendai.'

Hayasaka sensei patted me on the back.

'Listen,' he said. 'My wife wants to make you a warm jacket for the winter. She tells me to get your size measured, okay?'

I did not have the vocabulary to respond to such kindess. I apologised and said that I was not worthy of such attention, stumbling, and then in English reminded him of the stupidly obviously, that I had never even met his wife, did not even know he had a wife.

'But she thinks of you far away from your mother and getting cold,' he smiled.

Mr Moriya was approaching, fumbling his way at some speed

between the tables and the groups of people, scattering chairs. Everyone fell silent as they saw him coming. He nodded abruptly to Hayasaka sensei, carefully ignoring the younger teachers, and placed his hand firmly on my shoulder. We were to join, he told me, a more elite group led by Sato sensei. 'You had better say goodbye,' he said.

So I waved goodbye, and we left.

The air was cold outside and it was actually a good feeling to be walking fast through the night, both with and without company – for although I could not follow their joking, I could enjoy it. I walked a bit apart while they progressed in a bundle with their hands on each other's shoulders, bumping into each other. Sato sensei kept stopping to laugh, slapping his hands on his knees, flashing a golden tooth, and every time he paused someone walked straight into him.

'I think we are going round in circles, we've passed here already,' I said after a while, not minding at all that no one was listening to me. But Mr Moriya heard that I had spoken, and assured me that he would join Anna-chan in a song during the karaoke.

At last Sato sensei chanced to be concentrating as we passed by the building for the second or third time. He thought the bar that he wanted was on the tenth floor, and only half of us could fit in the lift, so I got in and held the 'open door' button while the rest of them went through the complicated ritual of deciding who should walk. No one suggested waiting for the lift to return. We rode up the outside of the building and could see to north and east the neon lights of the city and the headlamps of cars, red as they went up the street, white as they came down, like electronic ants.

Everything in the bar was purple except for the mirrors, and our group stumbled over the purple cushions, settling with legs crossed or straight out in front or even wide apart – anything but kneeling.

They were not listening to each other. Sato sensei pretended to be a dog, and barked outrageously, repeating, 'What kind am I now? What now?' Instead of answering someone approached him from behind, sniffed him.

More and more whisky arrived, and the song book was passed round so that we could choose what we wanted to sing. Under duress I agreed to perform 'Yesterday' and Mr Moriya told everyone loudly that we would be singing a duet, and in stereo.

A woman in a purple *kimono* came to our table with some strawberries, chocolates and more nuts, and laid the dishes out neatly. She tweaked Sato sensei's ear, teasing him, and he stretched his veined arm up her back.

'This is the best hostess in town,' he said grandly, in English, introducing us. 'And this is Anna sensei, visiting English teacher.'

We exchanged formal greetings over the heads of the men, and she looked serious while she spoke to me above their noise, asking politely where I came from and whether I liked Japan. I wrote a story once when I was at school about a lost man who had been forced to live among a group of apes in order to survive. One day he had met another human living in similar fashion and so great was the excitement of these two men that they had embraced each other and clutched hands before realising that their only means of communicating was through the gestures that the apes had taught them. It seemed like that as the two of us tried to talk.

'She owns this club,' I was told, once she had gone. 'But she is not too proud and she enjoys serving here. She likes to meet the clients.'

'That's us,' said Moriya sensei, explaining the difficult word.

'Really?' I said, trying to sound cold.

For a moment it was as if they had not been drinking at all and then Sato sensei barked, someone tipped over a drink, and once more they were released.

Mr Moriya, though, was not entirely at ease.

I watched him over the rim of my beer glass which I sipped at as if it held wine. He was restless on his cushion, and every few minutes he would shift a little nearer me. His laugh lingered after the other laughs like a smell and he wiped his forehead continuously with his white linen handkerchief.

'How about a strawberry?' he giggled. 'I know Anna-chan

likes strawberries.' He began fingering the strawberries on the dish in front of him.

I shook my head.

But he shifted closer still and with clumsy obscure movements seemed to be trying to feed me. He dangled one by the stalk. I put up my hand, hoping to finish the game, but he took it away then.

I grabbed Sato sensei's shoulder as I got up and begged him to come and sing 'Yesterday' with me. A feeble rebellion. Mr Moriya looked at the strawberry and then placed it delicately back on the plate.

'Do take my place,' he said, gesturing grandly. 'I can sing with Anna sensei *any* time.'

Later that night I tried to tell everyone about a robot I saw on display in a department store. It was a wonderful robot. It came up to me – attracted I suppose by heat – and introduced itself, asking my name and where I lived. After a few pleasantries it asked something that I did not understand, and when I said '*Wakarimasen*', it replied,

'*Nihon-jin desu-ka?*' (Are you Japanese?)

'*Ie, Igirisu-jin desu.*' And immediately it switched into English.

'Where do you come from in England?'

'London.'

'Ah, I know London. Big Ben, Princess Diana.' It sounded like one of my students.

I would have chatted on for much longer, but the robot noticed a crowd of people forming and presuming that they were waiting for a turn – perhaps rather arrogantly, for they were watching me with almost as much interest – it excused itself and shuffled off. I have an idea that it used the phrase 'I must mingle'.

When I went back the next day I was sad that it was no longer there. I learnt that it was part of a touring exhibition, and that normally it lived in a museum in Osaka.

I wanted to tell everyone here on these purple cushions how wonderful it was, but could say only very simply what had happened and my story did not appear to interest them at all. I used my hands in mime as I felt them slipping away.

'Say it in English,' said Mr Moriya. 'I will translate.'

'No,' I said, surprised by my own ferocity. 'I've finished now.'

Yet sometimes I was almost glad of Mr Moriya.

If Ishikawa sensei had been my supervisor, the colours of everything would have been different. An obvious point, but it can still be refreshing to think of it sometimes.

One morning when Moriya sensei was teaching a double class, Ishikawa sensei brought me a cup of tea, something he had not done before. Then he sat down and asked me if I would do him a favour by reading onto some tapes for him. He wanted tape recordings of all the text book passages that he was covering that term.

'Of course,' I said.

We went into a room which I hadn't seen previously, and set up the tape recorder and the microphone.

'It's just four or five pages altogether,' he said. 'It should not take long.'

I read it through once, and he watched me carefully, as if he was worrying that I would suddenly refuse to co-operate.

'That's fine,' I said, trying to reassure him. 'Shall we start?'

'One thing,' he blushed. 'Could you possibly do it with an American accent? You see, American English is the one being taught now.'

'I don't think I can,' I said, apologetic but cool. 'I think a fake American accent would be worse than plain old English, don't you?'

'Oh yes, yes of course,' he agreed. 'It would be worse.'

Mr Moriya would have appreciated this little incident, but I preferred to keep it to myself.

'There's a mosquito under my desk,' I told Moriya sensei. 'It's driving me up the wall. They always go for me.'

'The mosquito season is over in Miyagi.'

'But I'm covered in bites. And there's one under my desk right now.'

'The mosquitoes are all dead by this time of year. It must be a different insect.'

I had been trying to humour him but part of me stubbornly refused to help. I stood up and hovered around my desk, hoping the mosquito would get out. He kept his head down and his nose nearly touched the page. I did not for a moment believe he was reading.

He was sulking.

When I came in that morning he had not yet arrived, and one of the young teachers from the electrical department, emboldened by our introduction during the *bunkansai* party, invited me for tea in their staffroom. I had been before with Moriya sensei, and once helped carry some science equipment over there, but none of the electrical teachers had seemed interested in me.

I was wrong. They had been discussing among themselves for weeks how they might practise their English with me. Now, five or six men in white boiler suits bustled around bringing little cakes and biscuits wrapped in three layers of paper and foil – so that I felt like a queen bee.

'Do you like Japanese tea or Western tea?' asked the young teacher who had invited me.

'I think your judging of boys dressed as girls is good,' said an older man, coming to sit beside me. 'Since you came to the school, we have all been studying English harder. Sasaki sensei is the best.' He nodded towards the young man bringing tea.

'He was in England for pleasure,' added a man of about forty, whose face I would have a hard time remembering.

'London and Edinburgh,' said Sasaki sensei. 'My favourite place is The British Museum.'

'Ah, yes,' the room echoed, in both English and Japanese, 'The British Museum.'

I sipped my tea and unwrapped a biscuit, and unwrapped it again, and again, until it appeared.

'Do you like Moriya sensei?' asked the older teacher, Toyama sensei, throwing me a golden-toothed smile.

I paused. They needed an answer. In that lay the future of our friendships.

'He has been very good to me, but he is a little over-protective,' I said. I knew I was being too cautious, but I found myself suddenly unable to denounce him.

'We hear his wife makes you a *bento* every day! And he does not like us to speak with you,' said Sasaki sensei. 'He says you like free time, and we cannot take your privacy.'

'That's rubbish,' I replied carefully. I was on unsteady ground here. It was not entirely rubbish. 'He takes up an awful lot of my time.'

One or two of them understood this, laughed and translated to the group – and everyone was laughing when Moriya sensei walked in.

'Anna sensei must come to the morning meeting of academic staff,' he sniffed in English, then in Japanese. I put down my tea cup and rose stiffly. No one spoke. Something between us bewitched them.

I stammered my thanks, feeling like a child – a young wife being dragged away from a party. My heart pounded so vigorously I could hear it – see it – pressing out of my chest as we walked back outside and across the yard to our staffroom.

And he would not speak to me.

'I'm going to wander around a bit.' My voice was hesitant, as though I was asking permission to leave.

He nodded. As I walked away he called after me sharply.

'Where are you going?'

'I'm just going to walk around,' I said.

*

I went directly to the metal-working rooms. Hayasaka sensei had a class with him, making English anvils. He had miniature models of English and Japanese anvils, which did look slightly different, although I could not concentrate on his elaborate explanations for long enough to understand the finer details. He asked what kinds of anvil were used in England besides their own model.

'I really don't know.'

And he roared with laughter at my ignorance, thumping me, gently, on the back.

'Class, get on with your work – I'm getting Anna sensei some tea.'

A boy wolf-whistled. I knew him. He slept through my classes, but he always had a nice smile when he woke up. Hayasaka sensei was grinning. I thought, Moriya sensei would give an awful lot for this.

We took the tea back into the workshop and watched the students hammering and soldering – watched the sparks fly out and settle on the rough earth floor. It was comforting to hear the sizzle and spit, then see the sparks fall – resting softly on the floor for a moment, bright like a butterfly, before disappearing into the earth in silence.

The students who slept or could not answer a single question in my classes – even those I designed to make them feel confident – were the ones most in their element here. One boy I did not even recognise, though I must have had eight or nine lessons with him. He was polishing a small round disc of metal, making it smooth and shiny, the kind of thing people want to hold tight and perfect in the palm of a hand.

'It's beautiful,' I told him. 'Really.' And the boy nodded in understanding.

At midday I returned to the staffroom to accept my lunch-box from Mr Moriya. Most of the pieces in it happened to be my favourite things and I felt a bit mean for having disappeared half the morning. The tempura was delicious. I even ate the pickled plum which decorated the rice like the red sun on the Japanese flag – I wanted its strong taste for a change. Being sociable made me feel hungry and tough. Yet after half an hour sitting beside his silence, eating formally with our chopsticks, drinking the tea which I had made and offered him, I could feel my strength fading again.

'It really was a mosquito,' I said, feebly.

'It is not a good idea to visit teachers when they have a class. It might disrupt the students,' he replied without looking up.

The students I had watched doing their metal-work had a class with me the next day. The lesson went well, we all seemed closer, and there was a lot of laughing. We did pronunciation – the difficulties of 'rice' and 'lice', 'river' and 'liver'. (Someone had written in answer to a short quiz about me, that in Rondon I rived by the Thames liver. It was a better feeling once they could all share the joke.)

After the class, the boy whom I had not recognised before came up to the front and handed me the silver disc he had been polishing.

'Present for Anna sensei,' he said. 'Keep, please.'

It was cool and soft in my hand.

'Thank you so *so* much.' I touched his shoulder with my fingers, wishing I could hug him, and he slipped away from me as if in terror that I might.

I wrote at the top of the page – A collection of odd pictures. Then I thought for a bit and added – For anyone.

I was in a car the other day, I wrote, and I saw a new building with a large glass window-wall exposing the whole ground floor. Inside, a group of men in suits were surveying the room. One was walking along with his head held back, looking up, and one was slumped a little, writing frantically on a clip board. One was bent double either in agony or, as no one was taking any notice, merely checking the floor, while two more were engaged in a sort of dance, pointing first to the corners, then up, down, out at us, like the Pink Panther. Following one such point I saw outside, in the street, an enormous ragged dog, watching the show enraptured like a child at the cinema. Passers-by were carefully arcing around – less, I imagine, for fear of interrupting its view, than from the discomfort one feels at walking across the bright lights of a projector.

The lights turned green (or, as the Japanese say, blue) and I haven't seen the dog since, though I feel she will turn up again.

It is still very hot here, which perhaps partially accounts for my dream last night. I soaked the sheet, but this makes the room even damper and a few days ago I found mould creeping along the *tatami* mats.

Another image of watching. I was trying on some shoes in Ichibancho and was turning my foot around, pointing my toes, wondering if they were too tight, when I began to feel that someone was staring at me, over my shoulder through the mirror. I glanced up and saw through the mirror an old woman in a heavy *kimono*. She was hunched, frail, but her black eyes mesmerised me. When her daughter, a rather grand woman in a pink suit, noticed and bustled her away, I thought I heard the old woman whispering, 'She has the same hair, the same hair.' Immediately I form for her an American soldier lover – a long-lost Western daughter. Past that there are too many possibilities.

And then I folded the letter in half and in half again as many times as it would go, and when I unfolded it I wrote on the other side, across the creases.

I wrote – Anna is writing.

Above, the sky is still blue, but the sun is setting over the cliffs on the far side of the river. The television towers wink the last rays of light to each other, and the television sets across town are flickering on as the children return home from their clubs and their evening classes.

Mosquitoes are awakening, and begin to come to the lit windows and try to squeeze through the gauze. The lucky ones find a crack and push through; the clever ones lie low and wait now until after the lights are out.

Anna writes to distance herself from the day. She writes so that her loneliness might become positive, idealised or at some future date shared.

Her hair hangs flat, and her skin is blotchy. A mosquito has bitten her cheek, which has fascinated some of the people she has met today.

Now she can go through the window and float upstream a little, following the curve of the river, toward the centre of the town. She hovers over the bright lights of the pedestrian streets, and watches the people coming out of cafés, going into cinemas, waiting outside the underground station for the friends they will spend the evening with.

She does something she has always longed to do – back-flips from lamp post to lamp post along the streets. This opens up her chest, opens up the muscles on her back like stretching in the morning.

'What's that on your cheek?'

'I think it's a mosquito bite.'

'It doesn't look like a mosquito bite,' said someone else, coming closer and putting out kindly hands.

Please, leave it, she thought.

But she had not been able to say.

*

Her escapade over the town often leads her back to the grey office, the grey desks. The dusty tomes which topple from the right into her space.

She sets off again, up the school road, past the *ramen* shop with the blue and white banners across the sliding door. She passes the electric lights of the 'seven-eleven', and enters the park.

The grass is damp and smells like an English garden. Someone is playing a violin very slowly.

She moves on across to the very centre of town, the prefectural building. Kazuo had said, 'The park by the prefectural office has windows.'

'You mean, the *kencho* building?'

'No, the park by it.'

'And how come the park has windows?'

'Windo,' he says, laughing now and blowing his cheeks out. 'You know what I mean, windo, it is windy.'

The telephone rings. James is inviting a few people around to supper, but she has already agreed to spend the weekend with the Moriyas. 'Another time,' he says.

She pulls the futon from the cupboard and as it falls to the floor the postcard blue-tacked above the doorway floats out, down past her face, and disappears.

She sits on the half-folded futon and leans into her hands, overwhelmed by loneliness. Drums are beating in the distance, a festival, possibly on television. Before she starts to cry she crawls on her knees to the mirror and watches her face collapse, red, wrinkled, she forces herself to smile.

Later, she sits in bed watching a programme about the habits of bees, and how they can tell each other where the best flowers are through their complicated dancing. She feels that the image is symbolic of something in her life; it seems important, but she cannot understand why.

She dreamt that she was a small child playing in a park, swinging on a swing with a large plastic orange seat. Twisting around, wriggling, somehow her face became stuck to the plastic, her open mouth and nostrils unable to pull away from the surface. 'Mom-om-om,' she tried calling, but no one could hear. She felt the saliva in a ring around her mouth, and more was rising. She awoke to find her face jammed hard against the pillow which was wet, and as she turned it over to the dry side in her half-sleep she wondered whether people had ever dreamed of dying as they did so.

I found a note on my desk.

'Guess who my favourite character in literature?' it read.

'Is there meant to be an "is" on the end?

He pulled the note away and put a little pyramid before the question mark, and wrote 'is' above the point.

'So, can you guess?' he asked.

'No, I can't think.'

'Three guesses.'

When he was most desperate for attention, when all the other avenues failed, he resorted to a child's game, playing so innocent that to refuse him would have enabled him to win. I had no reason to refuse him. But I had learnt that the only move I could make which might harm him was to rush into the game so fast that it was crushed. Briskly, I asked,

'Hamlet?'

'No, but when . . .'

'Othello?'

'Ha, ha, do you think . . .'

'Hunchback of Notre Dame?'

'No, but close . . .'

'That's three goes, you'll have to tell me.'

The reason he identified with the character was related to Anna sensei, he said coyly. I replied that I had guessed it might be.

'Cyrano de Bergerac.' I did not know the story, so the climax was lost. As he related the plot, I sat in silence, back straight, shoulders stiff, face unflinching.

When he had finished I said steadily,

'I heard there was a film being made of it. With Gerard Depardieu. He played Danton in a film about the French Revolution which was my favourite film at one time. Have you ever seen it?'

*

76

There was of course a reason why the subject had arisen on this particular morning. That afternoon there was to be a meeting at the prefectural office for all foreign teachers in the prefecture. Mr Moriya had been asked to give a speech on Noh theatre, and he had chosen to give recitations from a play about an old man's unrequited love for a beautiful swan. He told me this slowly. Sitting back, I tilted the front legs of the chair from the floor and rocked for a few seconds.

'So you're going to mention me?' I asked stupidly, jerking back and forward on the chair like a puppet made from lead. I groped numbly for the place where my responses should have been, but couldn't remember what I was looking for. Or from where they might come. Vaguely I remembered the clam – that had described my self once – and I felt for its solidness, its softness. Anything to prove that I was not just shell masquerading as a live thing.

He had stolen my self, that was it. He was inside me and I had no room to think.

He was leaning forward, speaking.

'You understand now, Anna-chan, how much you mean to me?'

I brushed the spittle, his spit, from my cheek, and felt along the rigid indent of my smile as though it was carved into my skin.

Everyone believed we were going to an important meeting. That's what he told them. But in fact we were leaving early because he wanted to stop for noodles on the way and, if there was time, for a fruit juice in Mitsukoshi.

It was our secret, he told me, placing his fingers across his lips as we crept out.

'She is vegetarian!' he said to the waiter, and to the cook, and to the woman on the next table. I was silent. I observed the redness in his face, the moisture on his forehead, the shaking of his hands. The spluttering. He did not notice the silence and staring, or did not care, but talked on and on. I grunted when necessary in answer to his questions.

'Toothpick?' he offered as I pushed my bowl to one side. I

reached stiffly, and my fingers locked pincer-like round the brittle stick. I pressed its point into my gums thinking he must notice. I am separate but he is in me, I thought. I observe from outside, yet we are bound firmly together – and if I hurt him, I only hurt myself. But it is worth hurting myself.

In Ichibancho there were other people, noisy people. We walked in silence, and were frequently separated by the crowds. As we approached Mitsukoshi I noticed him looking at his watch and before he could turn to me I dived down like a convict escaping. He could not see me. I watched through the armpits of the passers by. He looked about wildly, confusedly, the crowds jostling him on. And as I watched, strength came flooding back to me, a smaller tighter self – my clam deep within – was laughing at the whole crazy scene, the poor old trembling man. I straightened, walked casually up behind him.

'There is no time for the fruit juice, I promised to get there early to talk to someone.'

'Who?'

'You don't know him – one of the other English teachers.' Sometimes it was so easy.

He did recite the Noh play but I sat with other foreigners and watched him through their eyes. He was shaking and the paper rattled in his hands. He wiped his forehead with a large white handkerchief (from England). 'I dedicate this recital to my own swan, Anna sensei.' He bowed toward me and I looked away, rolling my eyes, although my hands were clenched under the table. He was quite impressive at first, but he went on too long and people got bored, so the end was disturbed by chair rattlings, whisperings, all of which I appreciated more than the singing.

During questions at the end someone asked if he came from one of the major Noh actor families. He was forced to reply that he did not.

In these conference rooms at the top of the prefectural office, surrounded by Americans, Australians and one or two British, I hoped to find someone who might understand, but when all the forty or so teachers from the prefecture were gathered together I felt uneasy, I couldn't help distancing myself from them even though I wanted their friendship. When my turn came to exchange anecdotes no single memory, no action of Moriya sensei's seemed sufficient to justify my need for sympathy. I recognised elements of our relationship in comments others made, but no one seemed to have let themselves get entangled quite so deep as me.

Once I mentioned it to Christobel, an Australian teacher who lived outside the city, and she was very kind and sympathetic and sent me a 'definition of sexual harassment' which she had photocopied for several teachers in her school. There was mention of intruding on other's space, of phone-calls, and a clear paragraph on cross-cultural misunderstandings – but it was rather too simple to be of use to me. I never thought for a moment that I could pass it to Mr Moriya to read.

I didn't even know if I was making the whole thing up.

To avoid the walk home with Moriya sensei I ended up tagging along with a group going out to a nightclub. We danced under a display of strobe lighting which I would have been happy to watch on its own, but there was no possibility of talking. The room itself seemed to be jumping up and down to the rhythm, and we joined a group of young Japanese women in skimpy Tarzan costumes, fairy skirts and leather jackets. Two lifesize dinosaur busts protruded from the wall above, watching our writhing and jerking. Between their heads was written 'a Tyrannosaurus Rex and a Diplodocus just dropped in to say hello'.

I wrote late at night.

The old woodwork teacher laid his hands along the backs of mine, and moved the lathe up and down through my palms. I read *Lolita* at fifteen and thought I'd figured out what he was doing, and I said to myself it made no difference. I was even flattered at times, most people are.

Though once I had a terrible dream. I dreamt that he lathed all the hairs from my body, and called my skin monumental alabaster as he stroked me. But later red vein-fine cuts started to spread across me, and blood welled from the lips of skin that the lathe had wrought – and he threw me out then with my skin shredded as lace, saying I was just red inside after all.

I began to dread birthdays. In melodramatic poetry they became stepping-stones to death. I talked seriously of birth astride graves, relishing the newly found opposition within me, my own heaven and hell, my innocence and guilt. Obsessed by my perfect balance, and its transience, I was convinced that any day I would wake up no longer able to claim innocence. With only guilt, there seemed to be no possible energy. And no power.

I wrote, I feel awful this evening. I rake up unuseful things.

I wonder how the witty gravestones fit. I should laugh – that bridges distance. If you find someone funny they cannot hurt you. If you find death funny, well, probably you do die, but if you are not scared it won't harm you much. I write rubbish at this time of night, but I know there is a truth here I'm trying to get at.

I walked in a wood a few days ago, by the temple on the other side of the river. The gravestones were tall and smooth black, and they looked more like Death to me than ever gravestones do in England. In England the moss grows over – I hope it will grow over the new ones too, or is the stone too polished these days? Here the smooth black sparkles – the crows slip on it, and swoop away – they nest in the trees and feed on the food brought for the dead. The very first time I saw crows flocking here I thought it was the bones they were picking at, but that was not so.

He is not to blame.

To keep me busy he gives me gravestone words to translate. Or he teaches me *kanji* and my mind shuts down like the grille on Traitors' Gate, and I am swimming away fast along the Thames.

He is trying to be kind.

Today, he showed me a book in which he asked me to write my thoughts. He said he would ask me questions and give me topics to write about, and the first question was, What do you think of your Moriya sensei?

'I can't do this,' I said.

'But it does not need to be long – just one side, half a side – just as a memory you know. Maybe even *I* will write about *you* some day.'

'What do you want me to say?'

'Whatever you think about me – if I am a typical English Eccentric, or if I am surprising to you. Something like this.'

'I am surprised now.' My voice wavered. 'Really, I can't do this.' I asked him to leave it on the shelf, this little red book. I said I would write in it when I had the time.

I mark papers slowly.

I need to talk to someone, but even in English I do not know where to begin.

Ishikawa sensei says, 'Yes, it is odd he brings you packed lunches still, but it is kind of him.'

Sato sensei laughs – and oh, I do like him but he is so nearly blind – 'Moriya sensei is a happy man now, now that he has his English Lady.' He slaps his thighs, and tiny tears of laughter fill the corners of his wrinkly eyes.

During lunch which his wife had prepared for me he said, 'I have a plan for this evening, you know.'

I placed the chopsticks carefully on the edge of the lunch-box, empty except for the *koniaku*. The previous day there had been *koniaku* also, and it had stayed in my mouth changing shape but failing to dissolve, as if it was not food at all. I thought I would drown in the saliva.

Today he had plans. *My* future, I have my own plans for *my* future, Al Pacino had said as a young man, before becoming the Godfather. My throat contracted in preparation, in expectation. I could not see so far. If I got out of eating the *koniaku* I would compromise.

'I have a plan for this evening. I thought we could go to the English pub that I mentioned.'

'Oh.' I lifted up one chopstick and prodded it. It wobbled. It loomed up – pale brown, beige, semi-transparent. It didn't look like part of a plant at all.

'How do you like the *koniaku*?' he said at last.

'I'm afraid I *don't* like it very much.' I sunk back in relief. So easy once done. Its beigeness no longer mocked me but subsided into its rightful place, a piece of food again. Of course it did not have to be eaten. And yet I knew he had been watching me yesterday. He saw my retching. He saw how I fought to swallow, rather than accept his paternity. His generosity. And then he brought more for me, to see if I could keep up my battle. He would go on bringing more for me, until I told him the truth.

'Of course you must leave it if you don't like it. That is not impolite at all. I understand.'

Everything.

I offered to rinse out his lunch box – most days now I did this, as he provided the lunch. The piece of *koniaku* shivered, then rolled down into the bottom of the dustbin. I refilled our tea

82

cups – tea thick like soup and very green, for he liked it strong and I could not be bothered to remake it.

'So, how about my plan?'

Playing for time I repeated, 'The English pub?'

'How about it?' He leant back in his chair and balanced a pen between his two forefingers, watching me over the horizon of it. He knew I would go.

'Okay,' I said, avoiding his eyes.

We walked fast. He waved like the Queen to the teacher standing with a stopwatch by the school gate, holding his hand up as he strode on without pausing.

And he waved to the group of boys in nylon shorts who came jogging round the corner as we reached the end of the road. But the wave distanced, it did not bring him closer to his subjects.

We were going so fast through the University park that I had to skip to catch up. When I skipped he got even faster. I checked his feet to make sure he was not running.

It was still completely light but in the seedy part – the streets which ran behind Ichibancho – the restaurant and sex shop lights were beginning to flicker. The reds and oranges were drawn first to the lights leaving everything else softer, blue and grey.

'This is my favourite light,' I told him, as we slowed down, arriving. He stood straight with his head back, his finger pointing as it might toward the blackboard, frowning in concentration as he read the signs above the doors.

Even the air seemed cleaner, clearer at this time of day, and the new buildings did not look so bad.

'Here we are,' he said, lancing the air with his forefinger, striding forward.

I clung to the outside now that we had to go in.

The stairs were dark and steep, and it looked a long way to fall. Plumes of smoke reached up and curled about us as we descended. I almost laughed, it was so like being led into a picture-book Hell.

'It doesn't look very English,' I whispered.

'Sato sensei told me about it,' he replied. So he hadn't even been here before.

The inside was very small and the roof was vaulted brick. Perhaps that was the European part. Before the bar there was a felled tree trunk, lying on its side, supported by a metal frame so that it became a bench. The top side was smooth, smoothed by years of sitting, and you could have slid quite comfortably along it, only there was not enough space because all the customers were lined up there, perched along the tree, facing the bar. As we came in they edged closer together.

We sat at the far end. Whenever Moriya sensei got too close I slipped off and stood up for a moment, until he shuffled neatly back out of my space.

There were butterflies everywhere. Dead butterflies in dusty frames. Along the whole of the back wall behind the bar, where the drinks might usually have been, hardly any brickwork was left uncovered. None of them had much colour left and their wing markings were indistinct.

'We must have some *sake* – just a little,' he said, although he knew I did not like it. 'And a beer as well?'

I nodded and, because I was unable to think of anything else, asked whether he had seen the butterflies.

It sounded a stupid question, for they were everywhere and so heavy and dreary, so unlike butterflies. But he did not seem to have seen them at all.

'Beautiful. So, Anna-chan likes butterflies?' He was laughing, his outwardly affectionate laugh which made the muscles on my back contract and harden.

He poured me *sake* and then waited for me to pour his. I could not refuse him this, it would have been as easy to walk out into the dusk and leave him. My discomfort seemed feeble and unfounded. It was as though I had elaborated, exaggerated and so imagined someone who had never existed, about the body of a lonely old man. I could not refuse him such a simple thing – pouring a drink – such a usual thing.

But as I poured from the warm clay jug, he murmured,

'Ah, you are a true Japanese lady.'

'What do you mean?' I asked sharply.

'Your movements are beautiful like traditional Japanese, you

84

have an old-fashioned heart. And I too am old-fashioned.'

'What do you mean?' I persisted, but as the barman passed more beer Moriya sensei ignored me and began to talk about Guinness and pints and the pubs of Norwich. I turned my head from him – a form of protest from where I was sitting, up against the wall at the end of a tree trunk, underneath the ground. In a dark cellar with an old man whom I was fighting with my whole body.

I yawned. I looked at the butterflies and back along our bench at the row of men in dark grey suits.

If he touches me I will leave, I thought. He might just touch me, he has done that before, just a light hand on my knee – but not now, not with these butterflies, with these businessmen.

I could feel the alcohol softening, opening my pores. Once I laughed, and several of the men turned to look at me, and let their eyes linger, puzzling over our relationship. Slowly it came to me that Moriya sensei's arm was close around my shoulders, not touching, but his hand rested uncomfortably on the wall beside me. If I had risen he would have been holding me.

'I'm really tired,' I said cautiously, as if he held a hand grenade behind my back. 'I think I'll set off home now.'

'One more drink?'

'No, really, I'd better get going.' He didn't move. 'Now,' I repeated, blunt at last.

He moved his arm then and fumbled in his wallet for a note, pulling out too small a one at first. I rose quickly and began to move up the stairs alone, steadying myself on the wall.

Outside the street was bright with neon lights of every possible colour, and music trailed from each doorway. A woman passed, limping in her tight skirt because she had lost the heel of her shoe. She put her hand out to balance herself on a man passing by, but he removed it, coldly. She started to sing words that were incomprehensible to me, a thin wail – *Kayou Ko-oyu weee* – then paused, listening like a small animal. A man came up the street, shouting – red-faced, younger than her, his teeth reflecting the bright lights. He seemed vaguely aware that her stillness made his anger look ridiculous, but flashed his teeth and whirled his arms the more energetically.

I felt Moriya sensei push me gently from behind, and I leapt forward.

'Come, this way,' he turned me from the couple. It is possible that he really had not seen them.

'I can walk home alone,' I said, but he insisted on accompanying me. Slowly. For now I was the one walking fast. He wanted to point out a Burberry coat in a shop window on Ichibancho, and then as we passed Wagner's Café he suggested going in for tea and cake.

'You like tea and cake.'

'It's really late,' I said firmly, and kept walking.

The streets were full of drunken groups; there seemed to be more people out than usual. Office parties with one or two women who had avoided drinking so as to shepherd their male colleagues on to the next bar milled between pillars along the shopping arcades. Businessmen wrapped their arms around each other, singing. Some young boys and girls stood over a friend who had fallen and was laughing hysterically, refusing to get up. Her shrieking laughter followed us through the dark of the University park.

As we neared my house the streets were silent – the silence of families sleeping, of children sleeping. We were lit once or twice by the headlamps of a quiet car returning home. A child's bicycle lay on its side in the courtyard below my stairs.

I turned to thank him for the evening, and he tried to catch my fingers but they slipped from him. As I pulled myself onto the first step, he held his hand out to me, but seeing my face he turned his movement into a wave, not a Royal wave, but a real one. He looked just then a bit like Paddington Bear – that same solidity, that earnestness.

From my window the television towers winked to each other through the dark.

I pictured him walking home alone, sitting alone on the train as he was swept towards his home – home to all his life. I began to repeat in my mind things he had said that evening – all kinds of things. I heard him say that he wanted to climb Snowdon again, also that he hoped to visit a village church some Christmas day.

The England he loved was the one created in his own home, presided over by the Union Jack and the leather bound books – the England he reached through the writing carved on grave-stones.

I could not be a part of that. I could not understand how he thought I might be.

Miyo wanted to live in America. She wanted to talk about any country except Japan. As we pulled the desks together, making the classroom less formal for our English Society meeting, she said,

'I saw a game on *Sesame Street* yesterday which we could play – everyone thinks of a country and then says, "It's famous for *naninani*" or "It does not have *naninani*" and then we take it in turns to guess each other's countries.'

The rain was heavy and made the courtyard dark, but the light in the classroom was warm. We sat with our heads together as if plotting the downfall of the dreary buildings.

A pale face pressed against the glass, hooded in protection from the rain. It might have been Moriya sensei, who once asked hopefully if he could join our Society. Several days had been spent dissuading him. Sometimes, also, the old groundsman came to watch, his face always thoughtful. He saw English as a magical thing, a spell-language through which it might be possible to speak with the previously unspoken-to, even with people in his past, for he was still living partly in the days of the United States governance.

I only knew this because during the school festival he had turned off the television and stood in the doorway of his hut, waving a faded banner of stars and stripes. And I overheard someone saying that he thought he was still working for the Americans.

Next to me Hiro, the smallest, was writing on a clean piece of paper, preparing his country. He had written 'It is famous for New Clear Bombs and KGB'.

'Everyone ready?' asked Miyo in her bossy way. 'Who's going first?'

'And who is the teacher?' I ventured.

By the time Miyo had regained control, the face was gone.

We arrived early for the staff meeting. The tables were laid end to end in a square, with one side set apart a little for the headmaster and the deputy head to sit at. For once I delayed today, and he stood over me irritably.

'Need we go so early?'

'I think it is better.'

'I will just finish this.'

'I think it is better if we go now.'

The desks were cold and shiny, patterning and dividing the room. I knew the layout well from all the times we had sat silently waiting there. Our chairs grated across the linoleum floor, then all went quiet, except for the clock. An ugly pale-faced clock, which spent its days blankly ordering the room into thick whole-minute slices and giving no clue as to when the next cut might come. I glared at it.

'How about it?'

'How about what?'

He had been telling me about Alissa in *La Porte Etroite*. He had said he had read all the Great Works Of Literature, but she was his favourite character of all – of all women, he added, seeing my mouth opening to remind him of Cyrano.

Here we go again, I thought.

'Tell me about her.' Why not?

She was loved to distraction and for no reason at all she turned the love down.

'Oh, really?'

I was not sure what he hoped I might say. If I had turned my moon-face to him, under the terrible clock, and said – you guessed it – I love you, what would he have done then, deprived of my rejection? Did he think he was too subtle for me – testing my naïvety? Or had he asked what I thought about him loving Alissa all innocently? My heart beat extended to the minute.

I imagined I could walk out just whenever I wanted – I could throw the chair to the floor, smash the mocking clock-face. But another teacher entered, and another, and the meeting began.

His hands twitched his papers beside me.

One or two blue irises were left standing although most that remained were turning crisp and brown. The leaves were still strong and bunched together, spreading out across the water like a huge swamp creature sporting a few blue eyes. The sky was clear, and the water of the pond was so still that the gravel laid along the bottom could be seen patterning the mud almost across to the other side. A curl of smooth pebbles turned under the water and then rose as each stone in the line rose higher than the one before, and when the pattern broke the surface it became a row of stepping stones, continuing across – but only halfway across – before it sunk back under the water and disappeared.

A pavilion overlooked the far end of the pond and enormous carp roamed so close to the surface there that you could stroke them without wetting your fingers. Hiro showed me how to tickle the backs of their necks – most of them darted away, but one appeared to rather enjoy it and kept returning to us. It was just about the ugliest of all, fat and white with enormous whiskers, but it seemed to respond so well to humans that we couldn't help wondering whether it had been one – or, Hiro suggested, perhaps a dog – in a former life.

'Come on,' Kazuo groaned from the shade of the pavilion, 'we're meant to be practising English, not talking to carp.'

'Go on, talk to us then.'

'What shall I say?'

'Tell us a story,' I joked. And he did.

'There was once a little boy who lived with his mother and father, but he was not happy because his mother and father were always fighting. So he decided to run away. He ran away to the sea, because he had been there with his mother and father long ago when everyone was happy. Happier.' He stopped and grinned at us.

The fat carp flicked its tail irritably, demanding attention. Its drooping moustache made it look fierce, mimicking the giant carp which once formed the islands of Japan by its stirring – but as it fretted in the water a piece of weed tangled around one whisker, and the aggressive display was ruined. The fish dived deeper, and the thread of greenery trailed after it.

'The boy arrived,' Kazuo continued, 'at the sea. But it was not the same sea. There were lots of people and it was dirty. There was an old woman selling – dead – tortoises.'

'Dead?' asked Hiro dreamily. 'Tortoises?'

'Tortoises that go in the sea.'

'Turtles,' Miyo prompted. She drew a turtle on the earth, for Hiro.

'The tortles . . .' I glared at Miyo not to interrupt, 'the tortles were in plastic boxes, for sale. But they did not fit, so their shells were crooked – crooked? – and only two feet were on the ground, like this.' He moved into contorted turtle shape, then continued more hesitantly, quietly. 'It was sunny and in the plastic box it was hot. The boy told the woman that one of the tortles was dead, but she said – no, he was a liar. So he paid money for it, and carried it to the sea, and put it into the water. Then he went home, but he was thinking he was stupid because he did not buy – the live one. He – might have saved the live one.'

He finished abruptly.

'That's the end.' He gave a quick laugh. 'Was my English good? I told that story once in primary school in Japanese and the teacher liked it very much. She said I had a good head. But I am too lazy.'

'And is it true?' Miyo asked. Kazuo did not seem to mind the question.

'No.'

'Here is another fish which likes tickling,' Hiro said after a while.

We're only just beginning, she thought, to understand, here and there.

But sometimes I got nowhere, or went backwards even.

He phoned to see where I was. I was reading, pretending the hour to leave had not come, that time was not passing. But by then I was tense with delaying – the freedom of staying could not be sustained by the sour thrill of being late – a compromised pleasure. Not a pleasure at all. The words scrambled over the page I was reading, unable to reach me. I might as well have been there already.

And I had agreed to go.

So I put my book in my bag, optimistically, and took my toothbrush from the bathroom. I put on my shoes – the backs broken down, the stitching unravelling up the seam because I was getting tired of tying and untying laces. I sat on the doorstep to tie them, and watched the rain spiking the grey sky, spitting as it joined the swelling gutters.

'It's raining,' I told him. 'Is it worth coming to see the moon on a day like this? Will we see the moon through such clouds?' But there were sweet potatoes waiting for me, he persisted. And he had laid a fire in the garden for me to roast them on.

My laces were tied in neat, procrastinating bows – reminding me that I had left the chocolates I bought for Mrs Moriya on the table inside.

When my mother was a child, she took all the gramophone records out of their covers one day and laid them as stepping-stones across the kitchen floor. She only stepped in the circles in the middle, the bits where the tune wasn't. She didn't want to break the tune, just to walk inside the music.

I was thinking this as I stepped from book to book across the *tatami*, trying to reach the chocolates without my shoes touching the straw. Then there was nothing to tread on, so I stepped carefully, just on my toes, as if stealing wine from a vestry.

It was fifteen minutes since he phoned.

I locked the door and ran through the rain to the nearest station, in the opposite direction to the town centre. That way the cars drove fast through the puddles and the mudded water slapped my legs. Telegraph wires criss-crossed the streets from side to side, tying up the sky, and the buildings were grey and fettered with the scraps of old advertisements. A man's head had been torn away giving him the face of a monkey grinning through from the picture below.

The train was empty except for a very young girl in a purple miniskirt with her hair pulled up into tight bunches. Her knees were dirty, clenched together. When I got on she glanced up, her eyes bloodshot staring straight through my weak smile.

On the bus the driver growled at me because I did not have the exact change, and he was still growling as I got off.

The land at the front of the house had changed since my first visit. In August wild flowers had been growing where the wood once was, and the grass had been long. Now the earth was ploughed up and dark red, the last plants had been uprooted, and before the dormant seeds began to sprout again a thick skin of concrete and tarmac would be spread. The opera house car park.

'At least we will have an opera house on our doorstep, in return for the birds which used to sing,' Moriya sensei had once said.

So I felt softer toward him as I entered.

'*Tadaima*,' I called, to please them both. 'I'm home.'

Mrs Moriya came in a rush from the kitchen, smiling, bowing, offering me slippers as I stepped up into the house.

'I'm sorry I'm so late,' I smiled. 'I didn't realise what time it was.'

Moriya sensei came out of his study, wearing a trailing *yukata*, tightening the belt around his waist.

'Come in, come into the study, make yourself at home,' he bustled. 'Tea! Tea and biscuits!' He entered with me, then backed out and put his head round the kitchen door, saying in a self-conscious, almost apologetic voice,

'Shall we have tea, Atsuko?'

'I'm already making it,' she said.

The smoke of the garden fire twisted under the house and up through the wooden beams. The rain had stopped but the clouds still hung low, and I leant back in the armchair looking at the Union Jack – he asked if it was the right way up.

'It looks okay to me.'

The record player was working again after a long rest because no one had known how to change the needle. Moriya sensei proudly refused to switch to compact disc – he said sharp sound ruined the ambience. So we sat listening seriously to *Death and the Maiden*, sipping tea. For once there was plenty because the little brown teapot with the tiny spout had been broken, so we could use the Western-style one.

'He dropped it,' Mrs Moriya pointed to her husband, and then said something I didn't understand. Moriya sensei was humming to the music and pretended not to hear, but his fingers locked together tight and white.

I went into the kitchen to give Mrs Moriya the chocolates, and she was so happy she ran in circles trying to find a nice plate to lay them out on.

The one she chose had a green dragon curving around the edge, biting its tail, forming a circle. The dragon had very fine red and yellow patterns along its back, and the rest of the plate was a beautiful varied blue.

'This belonged to my mother,' she said, wiping it slowly so that the glaze shone. 'She was given it by a man from Korea, someone who was in love with her once.'

There was nothing I could say except that it was beautiful, and that was not enough.

'I don't think my father ever knew,' she smiled at me, and together we laid the chocolates out, then took the plate into the study.

It was almost like a family then. For the first time they talked about their daughter who was living in Hokkaido, studying music. From the fragments I could put together there seemed to have been some disagreement, but they hoped she might return for New Year.

After tea Mrs Moriya led me off to the bedroom and under her daughter's glowstars she dressed me. Even the under-*kimono* was pretty. Around my waist there were four or five bands, all pulled tight in knots which I could not undo, and then the *obi* which was twelve foot long, and wrapped round three times before being sculpted into a bow in the small of my back. Every movement became definite. I could observe minutely my breathing and the raising of my hand because of the new frame around me. Kneeling with my back straight became the most obvious, the most natural position. The material seemed to guide me.

I looked on my surroundings as a different person. I watched Moriya sensei's delight, and heard him suggest to his wife, not to me, that he took me out to find *tsutsuki* grass for the moon. 'But will there be a moon tonight?' I asked, standing between them, acting a child for them. I waved the long sleeves, winding myself up – creating the energy I needed to play the daughter for an evening. I was getting tired, my face was stiff with smiling. Dusk came and the last scraps of colour from the almost colourless day were being sucked into the gaudy lights of the town.

Even from the house we could see neon – the oranges, pinks and blues and greens of the video superstore near the bus stop, and the pachinko hall further down the road toward the station. In the distance an electric pink halo was forming over the city, guarding it all night until the pink of the dawn took the colour back for the day.

I was too tired to understand their talk, but kept smiling and twirling my sleeves. By playing this game I could free myself and them, our fantasies could coincide if I played hard enough, I thought, as I stepped down into the wooden *geta*, pretending not to notice the hand held out to steady me. There were figs on the tree, silhouetted in the dusk – the fig leaves and the fruit together could form anything, it seemed, their curves were so varied. The branches seemed to be dancing a message like the bees who told where the flowers were. But we could not

97

understand. We abused things, I decided – used things only to get closer to each other, or to centre ourselves, the same thing – a Union Jack, a tea ceremony bowl, a fertile fig, a fiery maple tree. We had no idea how to behave unselfishly, we Japanese, we British.

The vegetable seller's van was parked on the road, and two or three women were laughing over the size of the carrots which were indeed enormous. The little vegetable seller was blushing, and looked relieved at the distraction that I offered. They gathered round me, praising the *kimono*,

'And how well you stand, like a real Japanese lady!'

'How can you breathe? It is difficult for foreigners to wear full Japanese *kimono*.'

'We are going to find *tsutsuki* for the moon,' said Moriya sensei grandly. 'It used to grow everywhere here, but now it is quite hard to find.'

'Really? How interesting! How traditional you are!' And another woman said, with admiration,

'You make me feel so nostalgic. Wonderful!'

I gathered that it was not altogether a common thing to do now. I was not sure they even knew that this was peak moon-viewing night.

We moved slowly, me tripping and shuffling, with my legs almost bound together. Further up from the main road we seemed to be in countryside, and there was a barn filled with hay, and a small stream.

Moriya sensei opened his *kimono* a little, and brought out a pair of scissors – he had spotted some blades of *tsutsuki* on the other side of the stream, and I stood back, watching him stumble across.

He looked so deeply Japanese. In the dusk he could have been wandering a thousand years ago. And I was so English – English as the Union Jack, and the leather volumes – English as he was in his fantasies.

Yet he could make me more Japanese than his daughter, so he seemed to believe. He could return to the spirit of Japan which he perceived through the spirit of Old England in a bowler hat, and I was supposed to help him by merging past, present and future, old and new, blurring the boundaries of Nationalities and the shores of our islands.

I could help him commune with the Japan he was born into and the Japan of today. He had spoken through me to the laughing women. In the staffroom I was defined through him, but also he was defined through me. He was proud and shy on his own.

I thought how I would live further into the future than he.

I saw him waving a fistful of grass at me – or rather, in the darkening silence I heard the waving rustle.

The fire was nearly out when we returned. The potatoes were not – despite his promises earlier that afternoon – already wrapped up in tinfoil. In fact there was hardly any tinfoil left. He flung open the cupboards in the kitchen and pulled out all the drawers, while we prepared food and drinks, stepping over the obstacles that he scattered. Mrs Moriya ignored him absolutely, and so I did too.

'The cupboards are too small. I can't possibly fit everything back in,' he said, but she remained silent until all was back to normal.

Only three potatoes could be wrapped in the last scrap of foil, the rest we had charcoaled, eating just the insides.

'That's how they should be done anyway,' he told us, with dignity. 'That's how we did them when we were children. There was no tinfoil then.'

It was dark, but there were no stars. The clouds were thick.

'Where should the moon be?' I asked as he put the potatoes into the ashes, and he pointed up above the fig tree.

I had not felt so close to them before. We sat in the dark watching the sparks of the embers, holding our hands to the warmth, waiting for the moon. The *tsutsuki* sat by us in a jug of water, whether to attract the moon, or to be an offering when she arrived I was not sure.

We ate the sweet potatoes dipped in salt, and even the sweet charcoal tasted good.

'This is what it should be like,' he told us. 'This is what it was like.'

'When she was little,' Mrs Moriya whispered, but he appeared not to hear her.

'*Natsukashi*,' he murmured – more than 'isn't this nostalgic', the word brought both pleasure and regret, a powerful word.

'*So desu ne*,' she agreed. '*Natsukashi-ne*.' She pictured something different, but perhaps that was not important.

'*Natsukashi*,' they nodded together.

I brought a blanket onto the porch and curled up to wait. It was cold and the trees behind the house creaked in the wind, a lullaby rhythm. I woke at midnight – Mrs Moriya had put her hand on my shoulder.

'It's here,' she whispered. 'It's come.' And the first thing I saw when I opened my eyes was the enormous moon, streaked with thin strands of grey clouds which moved fast across its open face. Moriya sensei was still asleep. She had woken me first.

We were on the train, approaching Narugo, off to see the leaves 'turn toward autumn'. I sat next to Mrs Moriya, opposite the deerstalker. Moriya sensei sat next to the deerstalker.

'It looks as though the leaves haven't quite begun to "autumn" just yet,' I said, affecting innocence, looking out of the window.

'They will have, further up. Every year we visit, same weekend. Trust me.'

'The warm weather might have delayed them this year,' Mrs Moriya pointed out in Japanese – for the fourth or fifth time. I smiled conspiratorially. Moriya sensei ignored us both. He picked up the deerstalker, put it on in silence, and entered into his dream world as Sherlock Holmes.

The deerstalker caused havoc in the inn. When the maid came to lay the table for supper, both husband and wife had grabbed it from its proud and central place, failing to see that the other had it, and they were pulling themselves backwards and forwards across the table for an extraordinarily long time before the maid coughed, bringing them back to earth.

Later Moriya sensei went out for a stroll and lost it. Half the hotel staff were running around the village searching (if only they had had magnifying glasses), and the manager tried to detect where precisely the stroller had strolled to, without much success.

A young woman handed it in later that evening, having found it down by the outdoor spa where she had been bathing. Quite an adventure for a hat.

There were wonderful chairs in the corridors of the inn, which for 100 yen massaged gentle, medium or hard.

In the women's bath several bathers were washing their

children and Mrs Moriya insisted on baptising me as her own through her skilful rubbing, but the feeling was strangely comforting after the initial embarrassment. One side of the bath had a glass wall which had misted up but we rubbed circles and glimpsed the garden outside before the steam rose up again.

The water was so hot that it seemed to burn all excess away, and left me feeling that the poisons had gone, empty of bad feelings.

I slept with Mrs Moriya, futons side by side, very neat and clean.

The sunlight crept in early through the lines in the wooden shutters, striping us and the *tatami* without distinction.

Next morning we walked for several hours along the maple ravine, and although there was not a red leaf in sight (I was pleased to see that Mrs Moriya by no means let this pass unnoticed) it was indeed beautiful, a narrow cut in the land filled with trees and water. Husband and wife squabbled over everything, the names of plants, the temperature, where to stop for lunch. I posed for photographs in front of every waterfall, and in return insisted on a silence which made me feel as happy as if I was alone. They chose rocks to sit on and we drank Australian wine, hitting our plastic beakers together across the gulfs as the river passed around us. And the camera was passed about.

In the afternoon we began to climb up the ravine side and left the river to twist on. Mrs Moriya wanted to stop in a souvenir shop to buy *omiage* and Moriya sensei began to fiddle with a pile of paper lanterns, attempting to show me how safe they were in answer to an inanely conversational 'Are they safe to use?'

His hand had shot through two, the metal frames were spiking wires like disturbed hedgehogs, before his wife grasped one arm, I retrieved his spectacles (which had leapt to freedom on the floor), and the three of us marched out of the shop toward the train station.

He came to school with the photographs of the moon-viewing and Narugo. It was the first thing he told me when he came in, with a wink, but he waited until Ishikawa sensei went into a class before he showed them to me. I was quite pleased with some of the pictures of me in *kimono*, and I laughed at one – posed – kneeling on a cushion by him, my eyebrows crossed fierce as a Samurai ready to kill.

'There's a better one, the same but with you smiling,' he said quickly – but no, that one wasn't half so good a photograph.

There was me resting nonchalantly beside a waterfall, me thoughtful against some rocks. Then he giggled.

'Hey, this is me *sleeping*.' I felt my shoulders rise up. 'Who took this?'

'My wife, of course. I asked her to. When you were sleeping together in the same room, you know.'

'You *asked* her to?'

My arms were pale, my night *yukata* pulled up under my armpits and my face very calm. I had never imagined I could look so vulnerable. And now I was shaking and couldn't stop myself.

'It's an odd thing to do,' I said. My voice sounded dead – certainly so in comparison with his jollity.

He seemed to think I was funny to mind, and I began to think maybe I was, yes, I was – but still I was shaking as I stood before the students for my next class.

There was a chrysanthemum festival at Sato sensei's temple, and all the patrons were asked to bring guests. Moriya sensei and I were invited, and as usual the trip was planned as if we were going to conduct the Great Train Robbery or something similar. Maps were photocopied, then scrapped, and the laborious drawing process began.

A plain sheet of paper was unrolled like a magic trick, with a flick of the wrist and hypnotic eyes. He drew a landmark in the middle of the page with a curving motion and having explained what it was, he began writing its label, three words, then two more, and all five underlined.

I held my breath and turned to look around the room. A group were playing *go* in the corner. The clock ticked loudly, out of time with the deputy headmaster whom I could see through a gap in the shelves, slouched in his chair and snoring evenly. He might just have been pretending I thought – keeping out of harm's way – his head resting on his arms. Mr Moriya giggled loudly, and put his finger to his lips, treasuring my dreaming like a miser of tenderness.

A road was drawn, two parallel lines, and named. Then the underground station, named in capitals, and represented by a sketch of railway tracks running through a small box.

'This is where we will alight, as Shakespeare might say.'

'We?'

'I think it is easier if I come with you, and we can see Sato sensei later. It is more convenient for you, I think.' He looked for a moment almost embarrassed, he was seldom so unsubtle.

'Surely I don't need the map, then?' The game had wasted the free lesson anyway, whatever it had been designed for.

As a compromise I met up with Moriya sensei at the railway station closest to the temple, pleased that I had escaped the train ride because I knew how he savoured those moments on the evening underground.

The chrysanthemums were displayed under awnings and many had braces designed to help the stalk support the weight of the flower, with little platforms for the flower to sit at the correct angle. The stalks were juicy like an over-ripe vegetable, soft looking, going yellow. Some of the flowers were so dense, so full of petals that they could barely open but waited ready for the stem to rot and the petals to be freed.

Inside the temple an enormous tea ceremony was about to begin, and through the opened walls the kneeling visitors watched a *koto* player on her red rug, plucking out notes which calmed and made their crushed legs cease hurting.

The cakes were especially delicious – *ichigo daifuku*, pounded soft rice around sweet bean and a whole strawberry. Not a traditional filling, but then meat and alcohol should not have been served in a Buddhist temple anyway. Mr Moriya watched me turn the tea bowl in my hands, conforming to the ritual without thinking now. Then to break the moment, to show he had seen it, he announced in too loud a voice, half mocking and half proud,

'A true Japanese lady.'

I handed the bowl back crudely, asserting myself as a foreigner, searching his eyes to see whether he had noticed my insult.

As it grew dark the guests took their places on cushions around the long dining-table, and opened up their food-boxes. Moriya sensei began to hand over everything he knew I liked – little delicacies made of aubergine, pieces of crisp tempura – and in turn he offered to take anything I did not like, which I declined. I forced the rubbery *koniaku* down my throat, but it rose up as I breathed, and as it finally sank I turned away and retched.

'So you are learning to eat even *koniaku* now.'

I ignored him.

But he wanted all my attention. He whispered to Sato sensei, but I knew he was watching me.

'We are planning something – a fine secret!' chuckled the old man, and I had to smile and ask what it was because despite everything he was really a very sweet old man, and also host at present.

'Don't give it away!' shrieked Moriya sensei. 'She is listening.'

His excitement was making me uneasy. Beads of sweat gathered and broke, dampening his eyebrows.

Pretending I hadn't heard, I began a hurried conversation with a woman seated two cushions down.

'Delicious isn't it?'

'Ah, do you think so, I'm so glad. Are you a foreigner?'

I was sorely tempted to say, 'No, what gave you that idea?' but smiled through gritted teeth, knowing that the next question would be 'And don't you use chopsticks well?'

'O-hashi wa jozu desu ne?'

'A, so desu ka?' I half agree, using a lazy rudeness to cut the conversation short.

'We are planning a trip to a late season mushroom festival,' I heard as I turned back round.

Later some young monks called at each table, but I could only think of questions to irritate them – why so few women, eh? – and they soon unwound their feet from their robes and rose again. Moriya sensei must have been hovering behind us because he was right in there as they left the cushions, and he was much too close this time. As he settled he fell sideways against me, his nose half pressing my cheek, my lips almost touching his – a hand steadying itself gripped the back of my neck. I could see my eye inside his eye. My mouth was so cold I couldn't feel what touched it. And then I fell backward, shaking.

I had added a hundred tiny details together, each one of which meant nothing to outsiders. A palaeontologist who had recreated a creature through fossil particles and feathery clues – had been about to announce her grand discovery to the world – but still doubted the very foundations of the work, and dared not make her announcement. I stood up silently.

He propped himself up and replaced his spectacles, blinking. My hatred seemed much too much for him. My viciousness disgusted me.

And then I was seen standing there and was called upon to sing a song to the crowded room.

Everyone was so drunk that I did not hesitate for a moment. It was an excuse to be alone, raised up on that platform and singing as if no one else existed – no fake smiles or interruptions – as good as singing in the bath. No thinking, no past. No guilt.

I began,

> God save our gracious Queen
> Long live our noble Queen
> God save our Queen

and smiled as I let the scale of notes rise just audibly, bubbling up inside me. I felt at home.

> Send her victorious
> Happy and glorious
> Long to rule over us
> God save the Queen.

Cheering. No one admired the irony.

It gave me, however, the hard Englishness needed to insist, against everyone's wishes, on a taxi home – unaccompanied.

L ate that night, watching television, listening to the buzzing of the mosquitoes – for there were still some stragglers alive and well – I wondered why I had come here.

I had not thought clearly about it before, I had battered all such thoughts to the back of my mind. It was the only job I had applied for. It had not required making any decisions. And the same numbness was at work now.

I was scared of not living.

I had wanted to live outside Britain, but I couldn't remember why. I had begun to collect places like I had collected painted tins as a child, and I didn't want to get sick of the whole world like I was sick of thirties biscuit tins. I had wanted to specialise. I had wanted to understand. To live. And here I was not seeing or understanding or living fully at all, a rabbit frozen in the headlamps of a fast approaching car . . . I was the daughter, the child, the needed friend, the Romantic Incident, the biographer and the epitome of Englishness. I didn't know what I was.

It was my job to be polite. I was adequate at this. But I couldn't keep it up much longer.

I could not sleep, and finally gave up altogether, and invited the mosquitoes in, then leant on the windowsill sucking the cold night air like blood. Towards dawn I knew I was waiting to see how he would respond. Only when I saw that could I decide what to do.

I hoped for some sign, some change in him – *then* I would know I hadn't imagined it all.

After the chrysanthemum festival Moriya sensei refused to speak to me. We went into our shared morning class without discussing what we would do with the students, and he stood in silence waiting for me to read the register, then went to the back of the room, folded his hands, and watched. Some of the students looked confused and turned to see what he was doing, but he did not seem to notice – he might as well have been wearing a mask in a Noh performance. I did a long listening comprehension, reading a description of a journey which they had to put into a drawing. Turning to the left, passing some sailing boats and a man who looks grumpy . . . Some of them, the ones who watch my face, caught my glance to the back of the class – and their support made me bolder. I asked one of the girls to take over from me, and with a squeal of excitement she came to the front and I sat at her desk – she asked us to pass a disco, and have a ride on a roller-coaster. Then I offered Mr Moriya a turn, which he declined so sharply that the thread of the game was broken.

He retreated absolutely into his books, building a high wall of English antiquarian volumes along the line between my desk and his. The spines were lined up along the gap, so that I could not fail to see he was respecting my space. This was the only sign he gave to acknowledge my presence.

If he had cut himself off from the rest of the staff I would have found allies, but he had never been as friendly. And they took advantage of his humour, people he was often brusque with came and chatted to him, seemingly unaware of the cold black eyes that turned to me as I tried to join in. I asked Ishikawa sensei if he noticed what was happening.

'Perhaps he is thinking he should give you a chance to talk to other people. He would not be angry with you.'

'I think he is.'

'But what could he possibly be angry about? I am sure he is not angry with you.'

I kept my head down, and listened to Ishikawa sensei laughing at something witty Moriya sensei had said. I had never heard them laugh together before.

For some reason I couldn't bring myself to leave the staff-room. I felt I was on a leash that would only extend as I walked, which would become more painful as I strained at it. I sat numbly at my desk, keeping my eye on the barricade as the books mounted higher and higher. After three days of grim silence, I announced that I was taking a holiday, and set off to Kyoto on the night bus the same evening.

When I first saw Aki her face was completely white and her lips were red and swollen. I remember thinking that although I was tired she must need this break more than me. She was wrapped in a thick tartan blanket which reached her chin, and she did not move as I climbed over her to get to my seat by the window. I thought she had fallen asleep, and as the bus started to move I turned on the light and began to read for company.

As the bus thundered south into the dark I felt like we were escaping the city through a tunnel. I was watching my face reflected beside me, the lines under my eyes, when she asked over my shoulder, almost whispering,

'Are you going on holiday?'

'Yes,' I replied self-consciously, turning away from myself.

'Where are you from?'

'England – but I'm living in Sendai at the moment, teaching.'

'Really? I'm an English teacher too.'

'And are you on holiday?'

'Yes, I suppose so. I suppose so.'

We were silent for a long while after that. I was trying to keep warm under the thin green blanket provided by the coach company, but there was a cold wind – the plastic flowers above our seat were rattling about in their tin vases, and the clinking as they hit against the sides made me shudder. The flowers were dusty – as were the lacy curtains, and the blanket that I held. Not dirty, but not quite clean. I put my book away and turned the light out. Then got up to make some tea. Her eyes were open, and I asked if she would like some.

'Mm,' she said. 'I'm sorry, I don't even know your name.'

It was unusual, we hadn't introduced ourselves by name at first. I liked the informality of that.

'I'm Aki,' she said.

'And I'm Anna.'

'Well, Anna. Nice to meet you,' she laughed, and I noticed her lips had been bleeding inside.

'*Yoroshiku onegai shimasu,*' I bowed my head.

'You know you have a Tohoku accent,' she said. 'It's really sweet.'

'Where are you staying in Kyoto?' Aki asked when I returned with the tea.

'I haven't even thought about it – I came rather suddenly.' And I explained a part of what had happened, that there had been a drunken party, and now the atmosphere seemed a bit tense.

'I just had to get away from it,' I said lamely.

'Don't we all?' she laughed.

We sipped our tea in the dark – I didn't hear the flowers rattling then, just the vibrating of the wheels touching the motorway beneath us.

'So do you live in Sendai?'

'Mm. I have a family. A daughter and a son. Actually, I'm pregnant again.' She held the plastic cup with her teeth, the side resting against her chin, and I was watching the steam moistening her face while she was thinking.

'I'm visiting my mother,' she said. 'I would really like you to stay, if you would like to. I won't be able to be a very good host during the day because I have to spend time with her, but I imagine you might rather sightsee alone anyway.'

When I accepted, she didn't answer for a while, but put her hand over mine.

I awoke in the night to the sound of the sea. We were driving along the southern coast – had already passed Tokyo it seemed. At first I couldn't see anything but then through the blackness came the white crests of waves riding up against the sides of the road. The wind was strong and the bus was shaking in its determination to proceed, like some small animal fighting through a storm. The waves were alive too, like the hands of the sea reaching out to us – not at all threatening – as if they wanted to hold us.

We entered Kyoto as the sun was rising. I sat with the thin

112

blanket up to my chin feeling I didn't want to get off the bus –
wanting to go on past Osaka – to find somewhere empty.
Outside the window the streets looked just like Sendai.

'Perhaps I'm just sick of cities.'

'You'll enjoy it,' Aki said.

We were walking through mist, knee-high. The houses were wooden and low, with dark beams blocking out the light from the street and heavy sliding doors. Some had slatted windows but these were boarded up so there was no chance of looking inside. It was very quiet. The city was right beside us, around us – high-rise apartments on one side, and glittering offices catching the first rays of the sun to our left. But from this street we couldn't see them, couldn't hear the hum of cars.

The mist had begun to glow as we approached the house – warming, beginning to dissolve.

When we entered the hallway was dark, but as we walked further inside the corridors grew lighter until we came to a small garden courtyard at the centre.

'I'm home!' Aki called as we passed each door. 'Mother!' And then a woman leapt out right next to me from what looked like a cupboard, brushing her skirt down. She nearly jumped back in when she saw me, but instead raised her eyebrows toward Aki.

'This is Anna. We met on the bus and she needs a good home for a few days. And this,' Aki said, turning to me, 'is my mother, Naoko.' The mother asked two or three questions so quickly that I could not catch a single word, while Aki answered 'yes' and 'no' in a rather serious voice to each.

We made tea. The kettle was very old, heavy and black like the ones that used to hang from the ceiling over an open fire in the middle of the room, only now there were gas rings. I said that I felt I'd stepped into a different time with just a few of the best inventions of today salvaged. Aki and her mother seemed distracted, although they smiled nicely. Then Aki turned up the gas and said irritably to her mother,

'I don't remember it taking this long.'

'It has always taken this long.'

'I think you should get it looked at.'

Puff by puff a damp fog began to spread from the kettle spout, and Naoko – it felt odd calling her by her given name but she insisted – poured the hot water into a pot, swirled it briskly, and almost immediately tipped it out again into small blue cups. She put a little in each, and then added more bit by bit which made me think of dealing out cards because it was done so swiftly, so fairly, so that everyone got exactly the same strength of tea. It was unusually dark green, part way towards the thick, opaque, soupy drink served for the tea ceremony – and it looked beautiful against the rough blue glaze of the cup.

'I could show you the house now before the tourists arrive,' Naoko offered, looking me up and down. 'We have to open it to the public these days.'

'I don't want to be any bother,' I said uneasily, squeezing the smooth thick lip of the pottery between my fingers.

There was something between them that made me uncomfortable.

'Perhaps,' I said, 'I'll go out now and have a look around, you could show me the house this evening.' It seemed I had said the right thing.

I walked out of the sliding doors and up the old street; the mist had gone, and one or two cars had come. It was warm, although it was November, and the pavements smelt hot. I turned two corners and appeared at the modern heart of the city where smart boutiques were selling French towels woven in Indian and Mexican designs and scent shops had posters of Daniel Day Lewis advertising some cream for the skin. He would not do that in England, I thought.

There was a dress that I liked. I had not bought a dress for a long time, and I was almost tempted to go inside, but then the thought of explaining myself to the assistant, and of dressing and undressing and dressing again, made me move on down the street. I was searching for breakfast. That seemed necessary still. There were many bread shops to choose from, and I could not decide between a walnut roll in Ye Olde Bakery or a croissant in Marie's, so bought both. In Marie's I said that I didn't need a bag. I explained that I could put my croissant in with my walnut roll. The assistant pretended not to understand, but giggled irritatingly.

I knew it was not rude to walk and eat at the same time. When I first arrived I was told never to eat or drink in public – 'they think its *really* bad-mannered' – so like all new foreigners I went around for the first week hiding behind lamp posts if I needed a drink (it was so hot, so humid then). When the days began to settle, when the traffic lights and the different stripes on the zebra crossings and the heat became ordinary, I began to notice that Japanese people did eat and drink quite happily while walking along. Why else would there be one outdoor drinks machine for every fifteen people? That's another fact I was told. But we don't always put two and two together when there are too many facts.

Walking in this street I could have been anywhere in the world, and whichever way I looked memories of things flew up at me.

A year before, in London, I was eating a small box of sushi with my fingers while waiting at a bus stop. I was eating carefully, making sure that not even a grain of rice fell loose from my lips, but even so a woman came up to me and hissed,

'Put that away can't you, it's quite disgusting!'

'Are you speaking to me?' I whispered politely.

'Really! It's quite disgusting, and *in the heart of London* too.'

'I'm sorry.' But I didn't sound all that sorry. After all, I lived in the heart of London. *Unlike you*, I thought.

'Don't be so rude. Goodness! Just put it away, it's disgusting!'

'Don't *you* be so rude!' I yelled, and all the other people in the queue turned and glared at me, not because I was eating raw fish – however much that might offend them – but because *I raised my voice to an old lady*.

Was there much difference between our countries really? We were both just a series of islands, as Miyo said. About the same size. And with pretty obnoxious views about the rest of the world.

I came to the end of the street and I felt homesick. Once a friend of mine from America who lived in Tokyo told me that when they felt homesick they could go to Disneyland – it was a joke but needless to say there was truth in it. I flicked through my Lonely Planet guide and decided to try the Museum of Modern Art, knowing I would find friendly images there.

On the very top floor there was a sculpture by Barbara Hepworth and the smooth green-blue egg shape sent shivers through me, helped me, even, to retrieve that salty clam for a moment. The clam appropriated the colours and shapes of the sculpture as its own, as it appropriated the little disc of silver my student had given me. It was beautiful in me, no longer the not-very-pretty-at-all lump it had been as it lay naked once its home was ripped away.

There were threads running downwards across the smooth hole in the centre, so that the stone became a musical instrument – you can say anything about Art. A musical instrument singing to land and sea. The blue-green. The tea cup with a green sea inside and a blue shore rimming it around.

The trees along the philosopher's path were green still, but some odd leaves stood out red, heralding autumn. It was called the Path of Philosophy – monks, presumably, wandered from temple to temple along the stream before houses were built up on either side. Now the calmness would have to come from within, for the buildings were ugly and tired and crowded the water with their reflections. These days it was up to us to find the beauty. But then it was up to the monks too, I supposed, for beauty is relative, and has never been had easily. I wandered unhurriedly, listening to the water flowing, and the birds singing, and the gravel shifting under my feet.

On the other bank, I heard American voices, admiring an exceptionally pretty duck which dipped into the water, then rose, quivering its tail. I stopped too, and one of the men waved his cap to me.

'Hi, are you from the States?'

'No, I'm English.'

'Great! Our granddaughter is studying in England. She's having a great time.'

'Good,' I said. 'It's a nice place when the weather is behaving.'

They all laughed pleasantly. I felt like wading across the water to them, but instead waved goodbye.

A man stood at the corner ahead, facing the hedge. I paused for a moment, but the happy Americans had filled my thoughts and the sun was warm on my forehead. I glanced up at him as I passed and realised – my stomach tightened and my legs had rushed me away before I really understood – what he was doing.

He turned from the hedge, stepping forward, but I had

swerved, fast, stick-like, no longer aware of the stream or the trees or the ducks – my body was the only definite thing, defending itself from the world, hot, fierce – above all, alone.

An old woman in a *kimono* was watering a window box from an upper window. She straightened a flower, picked out a couple of dead leaves, and did not seem to notice that below someone watched her through a camera lens. But before pulling her head back inside she glanced down to make sure they had finished.

I stopped in a small inn halfway up the hill, so as to appreciate the prettiness of it all. It was crowded inside and the waitresses were skidding in and out of their *geta* as they passed between the kitchens and the raised *tatami* area where the guests were kneeling. I squashed onto the edge of a table by the sliding window, with some young Germans who did not even glance up at me – probably half the people in the room were European so there was none of the usual camaraderie between foreigners just because we were foreign. I did not turn over the menu for the English translation because I wanted them to see I could read the Japanese, but they did not appear to be paying any attention so I gave up and skipped through the English with one eye while I admired their camera with the other. It had something distinctly German about it, with its tasteful ikat strap and an enormous lens which looked like it should have been photographing the stars rather than sitting in a little tourist inn between two cups of weak tea.

A telephoto lens is needed to cut out foreground clutter, the guidebook said.

After my tea came, and the Germans left with a wan smile, I felt a little less uncomfortable about being alone and began to look about me. The walls were lined with framed photographs of carp, hung exactly as pictures of ancestors were hung over household shrines, so at first I thought these might be the dead relations of the ones I could see through the window shooting around in the pond below me. When the waitress came she

120

seemed friendly so I asked her about the fish, and she told me very sensibly and without trace of a giggle that some of them were still very much alive, and that they had all won prizes at shows throughout Japan. I wondered how they transported them, but the waitress was taking orders from the next table before I had got the words together.

So I settled back into being lonely and watched the carp slip through the water to hover beneath the miniature waterfall. The pounding water must have felt like a massage across their fat gold backs.

Where the cobbled street came to an end a dense scaffold of black beams rose horizontally, holding up the main hall of Kiyomizudera. From on top of it all Kyoto could be seen, and as I stood in the pink glow of evening a few neon lights flickered in expectation of the night. The city sprawled across the plain, but from above it seemed very low – merely a thin spreading rash at this perspective. And yet you could spend a life getting to know the patterns, the twists, textures, colours and images, of just one of the temple gates, so fine were the carvings.

The sunset drew people to the edge of the balcony as it thickened. A child cried – the woods behind the temple must have hidden gravestones, for as the wail rose black rooks which fed at the graves – on the offerings – swooped up from between the trees and scattered, then came together and looped, screeching pitifully.

The air we breathed was pink. It suited the love shrine, the lanterns of which disappeared for a moment into a pink equinox as their light balanced with the light around them. Although it was at the heart of the temple, the shrine was a Shinto one, and no one knew how it came to be there – a stone which guaranteed earthly love sticking its smooth head up through the wooden floorboards laid down by Buddhist priests.

A group of school-children in sailor suits were trying to fit into a photograph and laughing as they tripped over the love stone in their efforts. I watched drowsily. One of the girls seemed to be beckoning to me and I looked to my left, to my right, then pointed to my nose and she nodded. They welcomed me into their photograph. Another girl put a flower carefully behind my ear and patted my hair down.

As I walked back to Aki's house I passed the end of the street which is famous now for schooling young *geisha* but was once the heart of the pleasure district. The lanterns were all lit, red, swaying a little, and somewhere there was an out-of-season wind chime clinking mournfully which made me feel cold. A tour bus was parked outside one of the houses, and as I stood at the end of the street the driver stepped out and lit up a cigarette. Only the bright tip of it showed me where he was in the darkness, but he must have been able to see me because after a while I heard him whistle and saw the bright orange glow trace an arc in the air as he waved his hand from side to side.

Just beyond was the river, and on the other bank was a tall modern building, a restaurant. Each room had a wall of glass looking out across the water – and from the higher storeys the guests must have been able to see the lanterns of Kiyomizudera and the love shrine up on the hill. Most of the rooms were lit as I crossed the bridge, and I could see as clearly as on a television screen what went on in each. Perhaps two thirds or more were filled with the familiar grey suits and crisp white shirts of office party-goers but one room stood out, occupied as it was by a large family spread across three or four generations. As I watched, one of the children wandered away from the rest of the group and came to stand close by the window, accompanied by a very old man. Together they sat down cross-legged facing the river, and I could see they were talking and laughing as they pointed out into the night.

If you go to the Golden Temple, as all visitors to Kyoto will do, try to go in the early morning, when the reflection of the building floating on the water will look as solid as the real thing.

I left Aki's house at eight and not too many people were about to spoil my solipsism yet. Aki seemed very tense and I had been close to asking whether I should go to a hotel, but it seemed best just to keep out of the way. Her mother had showed me around the house the night before, as Aki had been out visiting an old school-friend when I had first got in, and it was the first time she had paid much attention to me. On the whole she seemed preoccupied. I had lain in bed the first night wondering what might be going on. It even crossed my mind that mother and daughter were lovers masquerading. But soon I gave up speculating and went back to familiar stamping ground – pondering over all the things Mr Moriya had done, trying ceaselessly to reveal proof of either my treachery or his. It always got me to sleep in the end.

The house had been an inn for samurai visiting the Imperial Palace. It reminded me of those cellars in which Q or H showed James Bond the weird tricks his department had devised. Naoko was similarly proud of the house's tricks, and I could feel her warming to me as she told stories of ghosts and princesses and vampire cats that had been seen within its walls. She told how the Emperor himself had visited once and liked the tea so much that he confiscated the land that the leaves were grown on. And a neighbour had the same problem with rice, so that was how one of the biggest rebellions of the eighteenth century had begun – through two households getting together to complain about the Emperor. Of course they lost, in the end, and many of them committed *hara-kiri* ('right here, in this room we're just coming to . . .'). And that was just the tip of the iceberg.

In the middle of the house, in complete darkness, her talking ceased abruptly.

'Naoko?' I whispered. I knew she was fooling me, but that made me all the more uncomfortable because it didn't seem right to be playing hide and seek with a smartly dressed woman of sixty.

'Naoko?' My voice slithered off pathetically into the silence.

All the walls were padded and sealed.

Alongside each corridor ran another, secret, corridor, hidden like a subconscious behind the wall. And I couldn't find the light switch.

I was preparing for the journey back to the living quarters, picturing myself turning down the 'ankle-breaker' passage where the beams were designed to break your legs if you walked at the wrong angle, when I saw Naoko's feet, then her knees as she lowered herself through a skylight in the ceiling.

'You didn't follow me?' She sounded genuinely surprised. 'It's particularly interesting, this part – a guard lived here in a sound-proof box ready to jump down on the guest below. It must have been a rather dull job most of the time, but secure and probably quite glamorous too in those days. Do you want to come up?' She was swinging now, resting on her elbows, but slowly she lowered herself and then let go to fall the last few feet, brushing her hands, brushing down her skirt and her hair.

'That's okay,' I had said.

The Golden Temple gate was shut. The ticket office wasn't open, and not a monk was to be seen. I could not glimpse the famous pavilion whatever angle I got myself at, so I just paced up and down.

Two tour buses met in the road. One hooted at the other to turn in first as there wasn't space for both to enter the parking lot together. A car slipped in between them and two old women emerged, and then another two, all straightening their *kimonos* which had been scrunched up, and when the third pair appeared I began to pay more attention, as one might watch a tedious magician whose trick had started to get interesting.

'It's rather cold out here,' said one.

'So it is.'

124

'For November, it's really very cold, isn't it?'

'It is indeed.'

'Shall we get back in?'

'Yes, I think so. It *is* rather chilly.'

School-children started to pour from one of the buses as if it was on fire, screaming and falling over each other. They were followed by a young man in a limp grey suit, who kept repeating, 'Quiet, please. Quiet', but the students looked like they were long past listening to him.

'Those children are rather noisy, aren't they?' I heard.

'Very noisy indeed. Shall we get back into the car?'

I remembered all this better than the pavilion, which sat, by the time we got to see it at half past nine, hot, bright and golden, just as it did in the photographs only it had a neat new fence around it. There was a rowing boat by the lake, on the other side of the 'Private' sign, and I wondered who rowed here after the crowds had gone home. It is not the kind of thing monks are thought to do.

The reflection in the water was pretty enough but left me feeling cold. So I sat among the bright green moss in the woods behind it, where there was still dew balancing careless of the gold pavilion, and a single red maple leaf like a fallen star, a harbinger.

When a child loves a parent, and feels happy in being protected and loved whatever it may do, this is called *amaeru* – passive love. The word implies indulgence on one side, and openness and trust from the person who is *amaeru*-ing. There is also a word for the hostility which the hopeful *amaeru*-er feels when frustrated from acting as he or she wishes.

I read that in a book Aki leant me, and for a short time everything fell into place – clearly, I thought, that is what he was doing.

He was wanting me to be indulgent. He was *amaeru*-ing. It was innocent and I would just have to be patient and under-standing.

But when I closed the book all the pieces began to wiggle. I tried to fit this and that into this psychologist's pattern, but the harder I tried the more fiercely the fragments which pestered me rebelled. I began to suspect that if I tried naming things I would make the scenes in my head more muscley. I might never get rid of them.

And why should I be understanding?

I leant back on the beany hard pillow which supported my neck, and tried to line up all the memories I had and to let them wash through me like rain.

'I'm not sure this appeals to me,' I said to Aki as she came to say goodnight. 'In a way it is just right, and in a way it is not right at all, and sometimes it seems so obvious that it doesn't help much to say it.'

Aki said she would come out with me sightseeing tomorrow, she had thought of a good place to take me and she wanted to tell me something.

'I have something to tell you.'

The sun was paler, moving closer to winter, but still it warmed us as it travelled across our faces.

Before us combed white stones formed the essential whirlpool, the essential ripple and splash against island rocks. A big stone rested amidst the waves, and one end of it reared up, spraying long grasses which grew underneath – a blind thousand-year-old creature with a mouthful of everyday greenery.

We were sitting side by side on a temple verandah, with our feet dangling over the edge, like we were sitting on a jetty by a sea only the sea had shrunk and we could overlook the whole world, oceans and islands both. It made me feel content.

'I have something I must tell you,' Aki said, and I raised my head from the sea. 'I don't know if you noticed anything, but – yesterday – I had an abortion.'

I was spinning, my winding sheet unravelling, and as I spun round and round I tried to clasp at the shreds of things Aki had said, the movements she had made, trying to bring them from the periphery to the centre. When I stilled, I wanted to crawl under the gravel sea and disappear.

'That's why you came down here?' She nodded. 'So it certainly was not a holiday.'

'Nor was yours,' she said. 'I asked you to stay because I thought it would help us both.'

To our right, over Aki's shoulder, there was a small round bush crossed with shadows from a leafless tree. The sun was fretful, coming and going as it did in England more often than here, and when it was weak the lines could only vaguely be traced, but in the moments when the light densed the shadows became as heavy as iron bars across the delicate leaves.

'Why?' I asked.

'I don't know exactly – I know it was the right thing, but I can't say just why. There were the obvious things,' she added when I remained silent. 'I couldn't have continued to teach with three children. And it would have been tough financially. My husband didn't want it. My mother did, but she is not always sensible.'

'What now?' I said – I felt so ignorant, hopelessly unable to help her, I let out any words that happened to drift up into my mouth. The events of the last months and the feelings lay like printed images on the winding sheet before me – flat and inconsequential.

'Let's go and have a drink somewhere,' I said, and took her hand as I stood up, pulling her up with me, and in my mind I pulled up the sheet too like a security blanket and put it loosely over my shoulders because it wasn't going to be that easy to get rid of, though now at least I had seen it for what it was.

'You know your mouth was all cut up inside, the night we took the bus? I sort of thought that you'd been beaten or something. I'd seen a woman with a black eye and a cut lip that day playing with a child by the railway station fountain. I thought you might be running away from someone.'

'I bite the insides of my mouth some days, that's all,' Aki said slowly, smiling but still holding my hand quite tight.

Jizo was a bald priest with a big grin, protector of both travellers and children. He gave up his own nirvana to rescue lost people – lost children who have drifted into hell by mistake, lost travellers who are far from home, silly and without direction. Aki wanted to visit the temple where he dwelt in the form of *mizuko Jizo* and offered special protection to those who died in the womb.

We walked along paths lined with little statues of Jizo smiling out from under red woolly hats, and dressed in baby bibs. Some had toys scattered at their feet – one, I noticed, had a water pistol and a solid tin truck, another had a toy cat whom I recognised from television ('Hello Kitty' she was called). The more independent-looking ones spread out under the trees, but many others gathered at the feet of the big Jizo like a thousand lost chickens trying to get under a mother hen, each with the same patient smile.

'I'll buy one of these,' Aki whispered, for it seemed a place to be silent. 'I wasn't sure whether to do it with the children once I got back to Sendai, but I think it'll confuse them.'

I read some of the *ema* messages which hung from the wooden frames near the entrance. Many just said 'I'm sorry', then Aki translated one or two of the longer ones. One explained that the family did not have enough money and the father had not had a pay rise for a long time. Another had been illegitimate, the mother 'a High School student of sixteen'.

The small figure stood firmly on the gravelly earth where we placed it, separate but with a very good view of all the others, and by no means alone. I was surprised when Aki opened her bag and took out a small baby's bib with a happy duck marching across it, and also one or two cheap cracker-sized toys, things that had been lying around unwanted in Sendai. It seemed strange that she had packed for the foetus, that its material luggage had travelled down with us on the bus that night – to me it made it seem too real, to Aki it was easier that way, like packing warm clothes and toys for a child going to live with its grandmother.

We walked over the bridge where I had stopped alone the night before, and watched a man tying his small boat to the river bank. I had just stopped myself from telling her of the child and the old man in the restaurant (all afternoon I had been trying to suppress a new wild urge to tell anecdotes about small children) when Aki looked up and pointed to the glass windows.

'I've always meant to go in there one evening, and I don't think I can walk much further today. Shall we stop for supper here?' It was as if she could reach right inside me and find that little cold centre and warm it up, making me feel that everything was easy, and I wished I could do the same for her.

'Yes,' I said dramatically.

'We had a rather foolish tourist here from England today,' Naoko said to me as we cut up vegetables for a lesson in making tempura.

'Oh?'

'He insisted on going into all the false cupboards, and he kept pretending to get lost, so finally I locked him in one and we went on without him.'

'You *what*?'

'I didn't have any choice, there was another group waiting to go round, and anyway he should have been able to get out easily, but he panicked and just sat there. He was nearly crying when I came back to free him.'

The black dog watched the surveyors through the glass wall, but she could never become a surveyor. I could never become Japanese, so I, too, might watch. That was simple. ('Oh, come *on*,' Aki groaned, 'you're not just watching, are you?') Fighting, watching, I supposed had not listening in common. Both were one-way-only roads.

On my winding sheet the images were not still as I first thought. They moved, they could be continued into futures that I missed. New meanings rose from their overlapping, magic-lantern-like, so people who never met, met, people who did not speak of their love, spoke.

We made tea, and I asked if we might sit in the garden, although it was dark. The bamboo water pipe filled with water, tipped and refilled very softly all through the night, but it could not be heard from the inside of the house, and I wanted to hear it.

In the small muffled sound of the tipped bamboo which led to the water's release, all things which opposed each other came momentarily together.

A bird that flew and swam travelled on down the river with its wings outstretched, to the sea. From under the water it looked dead, from above the water it looked alive.

The maple leaves were false fire, the cherry blossoms false snow. On our last day in Kyoto Aki and I visited a temple an hour or so by bus from the city, in the kind of village where foreign teachers are asked to judge the fastest pig competition instead of boys dressed as girls.

It was much less warm now, and on this higher land the maple leaves were just reaching their peak, shivering and rustling, reds and oranges and dark pinks which had never been named and never would be, because the season was too short to warrant such a vocabulary. Lying under the branches I felt as the Christians must have felt when they realised that the fiery furnace could not burn them, and sat back to watch the agony of colour, and felt it to be cool.

Winter

The one hundred and eight knells of the temple bells echoed through all the islands, in the villages, in the mountains and round and round inside the barrels of the volcanoes, in the cities and through the tunnels joining the islands, vibrating along the tracks of the sleeping *shinkansen*. The old year had been drunk into forgetfulness, the new year was waiting to be drunk. When the first sun rose I was asleep, wrapped like a caterpillar in thick futons and under an electric blanket which Aki's mother-in-law liked me to use. Grandfather brought us all the first *zoni* soup he had made in twenty years, and apologised that there was no well from which to draw the new year's water.

I took the stepping-stone track through the snow, passed the wooden fence at the back of the house, and continued down towards the river. The water was moving fast but submerged rocks blocked it, cutting it upright into thick sluices, and all the way the river was fighting its own bed. Steam was rising from a rock pool, forming a felt-halo of warm air before dissolving. I undressed in the pathway, and slithered down low into the water so that only my head stuck out, looking over the rim. Below the river crashed and bounced and fought itself, and on the opposite bank there was snow settled over the shrubs and balancing along the skinny branches of the trees. Then as I leant back further and felt the warm wet creep up the curve of my neck to the base of my skull – to my hair which loosened and floated outwards – I could see the stars clearly above, thousands of stars, as sharp as healing needle pricks.

I remembered the two women in Sato sensei's tale – the women who had sunk down so deep into the sea, through the silt in the bottom it seemed, the dark thick layer where they could only feel themselves from the inside throbbing out.

In the water I felt light – my body a perfect whole – I didn't need to find a centre to it, because I was the centre. There was no shell, no protective wall. Because there was no danger at all.

What was me spread out to fill my whole body and the whole was beating alone and whole and close to the outside world, trusting it.

That's how it felt.

The rock was smooth against my skin. For a moment.

In Sendai the first plum blossoms had fallen, and the pink flowers were kept fresh as they lay touching the snow.

Except for the small red glowing dome in the ceiling the lights were all out, and then Kazuo flicked the switch and an image of a child in a *happi* coat, on a festival float, appeared in projection, burned into the paper, and vanished again. There was no sign on the paper. But in the yellowing developer the child re-emerged, her face appearing pale beneath the ripples, watching while we chose whether she would be dark or fair, whether her features or the details of the scene around her would be accentuated. Then when we were ready, we washed her, arrested her in the fixer.

Over the years the fixer would corrupt and change our picture, distorting with brown amoeba shapes, it would eat the image, until one day it would disappear. But no one knew, Kazuo said, how long a photograph could last.

I taught him English, he taught me photography. He told me one day about an idea he had for a new form of art. A moving portrait. He asked me if it had been done before, and I did not know. A moving picture with musicians or a street scene in the background, and the main subject still or moving or talking, depending on what mood the picture was showing. But through this method it would be easy to depict all kinds of things at once. 'Someone will do it before me, however,' he said.

Often our sessions would end with a familiar rapping at the door.

'Anna san? Are you in there?' an agitated voice would call, and I would reply that I was indeed.

'Come out for a moment, please.'

'Why?' I might say, sweetly.

'Come, please.'

Then I would whisper my goodbye to Kazuo and slip into the cold evening, to be led back into the staffroom.

'I thought you might be wanting to get away. It's getting late. I know you do not like to stay too late at school, and it is right – you are here to enjoy, not just to work after all.'

'I wasn't working.' My voice frigid. 'I was enjoying myself.'

'And who was there?' He tried to sound casual. 'Kazuo?' I nodded. 'And who else?'

'Does it matter?' I snapped, slapping my books together, hugging them tight against me. 'Right. I'm setting off.'

Sometimes he would ask me out for a drink. Sometimes he marched out with me into the icy courtyard, and then the only sound was the crunching of our soles on the brittle ground. We would stride out of the gate together, turning like sentinels one left and one right, curtly nodding our goodnight.

'It's a bad time to have kittens.'

I had heard the voice earlier, but did not think he spoke to me. Now I turned and saw Watanabe sensei holding a small white scrap of a cat. Its legs dropped through his fingers and paddled in the air.

Watanabe sensei worked in the office with Hayasaka sensei, next to the metal-working room, but although I knew who he was we had never spoken together.

'It's a bad time to have kittens.'

'Might it die?' I asked, searching for words. 'But the snow is going, winter is going.'

The eyes were not even opened. I assumed he had found it without a mother, or else why would he take it away, it being so small? Though now he beckoned me and carried it back to the shed – the old shed, the only building to survive from the days before the war – where a cat had made her home. She hissed when we stepped up inside, and Watanabe sensei apologised to her in a whisper and put his finger to his lips.

'How many are there?'

'Four or five. One has died already.'

'Are you feeding her?'

'Of course,' he laughed. We stood side by side, stamping our feet on the frozen dirt of the games field and blowing our hands, trying to think of something to say.

'If one survives, you could take it back to England when you go.'

'*Fuku wa uchi, oni wa soto*,' I repeated, sowing peanuts along the corridor, around my bedroom, between the desk and the piano. We chanted as we scattered – 'Good luck in, devils out – *fuku wa uchi, oni wa soto*.'

'Is that enough?'

'A few more.'

I was getting less careful about crunching the ones we had already dropped, it was becoming so hard to find a free space to stand in. I crushed another shell, feeling it give under my slipper – a satisfying little crack – but I did not feel the same feverishness that I would have felt doing such a thing several months earlier. These days I was calmer, I thought. I enjoyed it.

Mrs Moriya had been watching us, her hands on her hips.

'I think that *is* enough,' she frowned. 'You are both making rather a mess.'

'Okay,' he said at last. 'Now, where are the masks?'

There were three, one for each of us, a red, a blue and a green. He asked me to choose one. The red one had a particularly sly smile, but he must have believed me mad if he thought I could possibly want one more than any other.

'Any will do,' I said evenly.

We were celebrating the end of winter although the ground was still frozen, but more than that I did not understand – and increasingly suspected that there was little *to* understand – that we wore these masks simply because you could buy them in the shops that week.

'Is this right?' asked Mrs Moriya as we picked up the nuts once all the devils had paused to feed on them.

'It used to be beans, but you can use peanuts now.'

'I mean, should we be gathering up the nuts while we are still wearing our masks?' I looked up at them with interest because she seemed to be fooling him. We both watched through our masks, devils struck silent by the serious child whom we had thought too old to believe in its game.

'Yes.' He gave nothing away.

'Wait,' Mrs Moriya said, 'don't throw them in the garden, I'll fetch a bag.'

And so it was that the nuts which held a year's worth of evil and misfortune were replaced in the food cupboard – and the broken ones were swept up and tipped into the swing bin.

Mrs Moriya wanted her daughter, not me, but her daughter had not come down at New Year as she had hoped, so I said that I would visit her and make sure she was alright. That was one reason for going up to Hokkaido, and the other was to see the famous snow sculptures. I took the daughter's photograph as well as her address and the telephone number of the student hostel where she lived, and I took a book about the Ainu written by a Canadian anthropologist to read on the boat.

I decided that if I got lonely I would write a short story about being Ainu.

I wouldn't flatter Mr Moriya by writing about him.

'Are there often baths like this on boats?' I asked the woman next to me as we sat looking out of the steamy portholes into the sea. Only it must have sounded more like 'Is it normal to wash on a boat' because she gave me a rather disdainful 'of course' and paddled off.

When I asked why all the food in the restaurant was Italian-style, the woman at the till snapped, 'What do you expect?' I couldn't think of anything to say.

So I hadn't found anyone to keep me company, but I still liked the boat. I walked up and down the port side corridor as if I was passing through an Agatha Christie film, and sat between two enormous ferns whose tips touched along the back of my wicker armchair. I thought of other boats I had been on – my old favourite the *Viking Valiant*, which was much nicer than its sister ship the *Viking Somethingelse* – and a boat to Turkey on which, so family history had it, there was nothing to eat but apricot jam – and sailing from Venice to Alexandria during Fergie and Andrew's marriage. An Australian had come up to us and said, 'Hey, are you *English*? And you go on holiday during *this*?' and we didn't know whether she was joking.

And here I was travelling again.

I consoled myself with the idea of a short story series. Stories of Japanese lives.

'Are you visiting for long?' An old woman with a very round, cheery face came up to me and sat down on the other side of the fern to my left.

'No, only two nights, then I have to go back to *work*.' But she did not look as though she minded a bit whether I was a straightforward tourist or a lunatic looking for the moon.

'That's nice. So you'll get to see the snow sculptures?'

'Yes.'

'That's nice.'

We sat on, watching the sea plash gently up the windows like upside down rain.

'I don't suppose you are Ainu, are you?' I didn't think she was the type to mind a question like this, but I looked serious and polite all the same.

'As a matter of fact my mother was, but she died when I was a small child. I was not brought up as an Ainu,' she said.

I nodded and smiled, hoping she might expand – I wasn't sure precisely what I wanted to ask – but she just nodded and smiled too, and we fell silent again.

I phoned the Moriyas' daughter as soon as I arrived, watched over by a transparent Samurai with sword raised, a frozen ghost, whose nose was beginning to drip, whose fierce scowl would soon smooth over and melt. She wasn't in, so I went to find a hotel, and read curled up by the fan heater – and I wrote.

Of course I can write as if I was Japanese myself.

The old woman who sells animals made from *kimono* rags, laying them out on an ark of cloth outside Shinjuku station – I could write as if I was her and hold my purple donkey and red horse out to the passers-by. It would be easy to mimic her mumblings as if these were her thoughts – 'Spirits from the past! Come, see how the Mongolian horse . . . See your grand-mother's wedding robes filled with new life . . . ' Or to be the well-dressed business woman who pauses to choose a fat caterpillar for her two-year-old son, and thinks, 'What a won-derful idea!' while walking home between the forty-storey towers.

But what would I achieve by pretending to be Japanese? What does Moriya sensei feel when he lies at night imagining he is English? How differently do we think? For I can feel his pain when I say, 'I acted *Romeo and Juliet* with my sister when I was nine years old . . . I went to the Lake District *years* ago.'

My pretence is the coldest thing.

'Are you a foreigner?' the little boy asks, edging forward.
'No, I am Japanese,' I say softly. 'Don't I look Japanese?'
'Not really,' says the biggest one.
But the smallest one is scared.
'Are you sure you are Japanese?'

Then can I pretend to think in a language that I barely understand? In a few years' time I will not allow myself such arrogance.

The baby by the drinks machine cries when I walk up beside him.

'Mummy, it's a foreign person! Quick! A foreign person!'

The old woman in the park with her great-grandchild whispers,

'Look, little one, look at the ducks,' and just now, gently, 'Look, look, a foreigner.'

Sometimes, to pretend makes me forget my Martian status, my green skin.

Going beyond this, beyond language, we can hold hands from our stomachs, and then it becomes clear momentarily – the world of imposing and being imposed upon. Flea-like truth which, as we put our finger on it, is gone.

Aki tells her own versions of Cinderella and Hansel and Gretel to her children. Sometimes the endings are happy, sometimes sad. She tells me to play with the folk tales for fun, 'As if they are things you see in the street, that is what they are.'

When I got up the next morning my breath formed clouds through the small room, and in the corridors of the hotel people were saying how cold it had become, just as the previous day they had all been remarking how warm it was, for the time of year. The receptionist was wearing fluffy white mufflers like rabbits' tails over her ears.

I found the phone-box overlooked by the Samurai, who had toughened up overnight, and his nose no longer dripped. He scowled at me as I dialled.

'Oh, yes. They wrote about you.' Her voice was cautious.

'I'm in Sapporo.'

There was a pause. 'I'm rather busy today – how long will you be here for?'

'I leave tomorrow around midday.'

'How about meeting for breakfast tomorrow?'

I paced up and down the ice sculpture boulevard, surrounded by nearly invisible angels, horses, warriors, Snow White with two of her dwarves and a Ninja Turtle. There were a lot of sheep too, it being the year of the sheep, but the sculptors had not been very imaginative, so most of them were hanging around looking – as you might imagine – sheepish, and I was hanging around with them. Unlike the spectacular rearing horse, with such a proud face that I regretted seeing the metal bones in its back legs, the sheep were spineless – but then they weren't cheating.

When I moved amidst this world of ice I felt like the Snow Queen – distanced, potentially cruel, cruder than my subjects.

There was a half scale model of the Reichstag, and a Triumphal Arch.

There was a massive Chibi Maruko chan with her arms stretched wide, gathering together her furry friends, and children were now beginning to climb up the snow stairway to her knees, to scream as they slid back down. The loudspeakers on their long posts started to choke, then bloom into life like strange flowers towering over us.

There was an American woman saying to her husband, 'My, oh my!'

So I went back to the hotel to write a story.

The month the *Titanic* sank, April 1912, my grandmother got a little sister, Misao. When Misao married a Russian and went to live in America my grandmother would say that she had been given the spirit of one of the children who had drowned. She didn't really believe in reincarnation, but people said that if a very young baby died it should be buried by the outdoor toilets or under the doorstep so that its spirit might return to the parents and be reborn. If a child was buried in a graveyard it would not find its way back to the living.

The family made a cradle for Misao out of wood. It had to be a special wood, because some kinds were hard and might hurt the baby. Maple gave a good wood with good spirit, and if you cut it sweet juice oozed out. Ume, my grandmother, was taken out by her young uncle, and they searched all day for the softest tree with the sweetest juice. They cut the trees with a knife and when the liquid swelled up my grandmother would put out her tongue and lick the trunk, feeling the rough bark and then the smoothness of the sap. Her child-saliva healed the tree.

The cradle was made of two flat boards which were pegged onto wooden slats. It was hung from the ceiling by ropes. A rush mat was tied to the boards and Misao was fastened to her cradle by a cord which criss-crossed her body. Ume could lie down and put her head under it. Sometimes she would poke Misao through the crack between the two boards when no one was looking. When the baby cried she would pull the rocking string to quieten her, and everybody would say how lucky Misao was to have such a kind big sister.

My grandmother tells me the story of the one-eyed baby – of Amo who takes a friend's child up into the mountains to gather wild plants. Other girls come too – they are all dancing – it is summer, the snows have finally gone, the flowers and the plants gather thick in every ravine and mat together along the pathway. Across the sky a stray white cloud unfolds ribbon-like.

The baskets are nearly full; the girls start filling even their headscarves and their cloaks and their boots. Amo is walking ahead with the sleeping baby on her back – the baby balances on a wooden stick and the ends of the stick are tied to a strap which reaches across Amo's forehead. My grandmother carried the sisters born after Misao in this way – her forehead pressed against the strap.

Amo is ahead – and then she sees a rock blocking the pathway which looks like a crouching man. Huge, grey, still it sits. The valleys and mountains around are beautiful, and the voices of her friends are not far off, but she cannot move. At the top, where the head must be, one single eye opens and glints at her.

The others come round the corner and their singing stops. When the silence is broken by the baby's crying they drop the plants and run.

Amo's first child is born with only one eye in the middle of its forehead, one little, multicoloured sparkling thing like a jewel set in a soft crown. Amo is so afraid that she leaves the child in a corner of her house until it dies. She feels the eye watching her until neighbours carry the little body outside and bury it.

'Humans and rocks and animals and plants interlinking!' snorted my grandmother, reading a newspaper one morning. 'As if it's a new idea! Has anyone been arguing that they are not connected?'

I am lying with my head on her knees, listening to the fire and feeling warm despite the ten feet of snow covering the earth outside. My stomach is beginning to swell.

'Don't eat octopus,' laughs an old friend. 'Or it will be born bald you know. Once a cousin of mine was expecting a child and she hated octopus, so she would boast about the hair her child would have. When her baby was born it remained bald for months and months and she would storm around the village demanding to know who had fed her in her sleep.'

Even the fire laughs. Each old eye glitters.

I know my child will not be Ainu in the same way, we all know it, and some care and some do not.

'My dear, we replaced others you know. We were the hairy invaders once, to the ones who lived underground. Some people think we killed them all, but more likely we did to them what others do to us. Marry. Forget. Like a season changing.'

I cannot argue with this. I do not know.

'At least the Japanese have no rigid beliefs – thinking there is only one solution – that is all you of the next millennium have to fear.'

'I think it will be a beautiful time, if everyone listens . . . ' Misao whispers into my stomach. 'Just you listen to us!' And she feels for the kick of response.

Misao. Misao who had not visited her birthplace for forty years has returned. She went to America when she was eighteen with a young Russian sailor. They came back to Japan ten years later when he, a naval officer, was stationed in Yokohama. They had one child who could not even speak Japanese, certainly knew no Ainu. Charlotte. Charlotte, my mother's cousin, whom I have never seen. They were not welcomed then.

Ume and Misao had never liked each other much, or had never found how to express their love.

'Just three years between us but so much was changing between our births, and she was like someone from another century to me,' my grandmother once said.

'But they were cruel,' Misao tells me. She speaks with blank eyes about her first memories. A bear cub had been raised in the family alongside her, found days after her birth, and she remembers as a two-year-old child being held in the bear's arms.

'Ume was so jealous of it!' smiles Misao, and there is a flickering in her eyes, something rekindling.

The bear cub was with the family for three years, and then it was time for the 'Iomande' ritual, Misao told me. She told me of the frozen boughs, the taut air, and the rhythmic music. The bear's muscles stiff, his hair standing up around his neck, his soft brown ears hardened and alert. He clawed the snow as he was dragged away. She followed until she reached a crowd of people and there, as the men passed through with the struggling bear, an arm held her back, a voice said, 'You want to go to heaven too, little one?'

But although she said yes, the voice took no notice, and she snarled and kicked and screamed (hearing the bear's whining), trying to get through the padded legs of the crowd.

My grandmother remembers that Misao would wake up in the night shrieking, and once she threw up blood.

I do not think the 'Iomande' festival was cruel, and yet I am glad it does not happen now. My grandmother gets irritated and rises muttering that worse things have been done than sending an immortal bear back to its ancestors, and she asks if we haven't got better things to worry about.

We sit by the fire, watching my stomach grow, Ume and Misao coming together after seventy years.

In 1872, or thereabouts, a group of boys and girls were sent to school hundreds of miles away in Tokyo. One girl and one boy escaped together and took many years to work their way home. By the time they arrived they had had a child together, whom they named 'Breath'. Everyone loved this boy who meant so much, but my great-grandmother had won him.

They look so beautiful as they talk about their parents.

'My child will bring the best of you together, gentle, tolerant . . . ' I call out much too loudly, much too sentiment-ally, and the two old women laugh at me.

I speak to Charlotte over the telephone, excited, because she is from my mother's generation and despite her distance I some-times see her as my mother whom I do not have.

'So is it a boy or a girl?'

'Well – ' I will always enjoy this pause, 'both!'

She shrieks and I hear her shouting it over her shoulder to her enormous family, part Ainu, part Russian–Americans.

'Oh my dear,' she returns to the line, 'I'm so *pleased* for you.'

And it seems like she has shouted it round the world – that the world is pleased that two new Ainu have, after so long a journey, with so unpredictable a future, entered it.

'Are you Anna?' I held out my hand. 'Nice to meet you, at last.'

Something in her features reminded me of both her parents. She had the glimmer in her eye that Mrs Moriya had when she seemed to be teasing her husband, the quizzical look I was never quite sure about. And she had her father's enthusiasm, but in calmness. She told me that her last visit to Sendai had made her close up inside, had made her unable to write music or study for months, so now she would not return until after her final exams. I could not ask her more. We were only together while we drank coffee, and I was awkward as a cuckoo talking of her parents – talking of her father was impossible, yet he was at the front of my mind, and hers, I think. I mentioned the glow-stars, and she laughed at that, then said that the night she put them up she had wanted to die. She made a joke of it.

I never got to know why.

One weekend Aki and I rode our bicycles along the raised paths between the rice-fields which spread from the city to the sea. This countryside was pressed like a giant waffle for miles, as ordered by humanity as the most structured town, but deserted. The sand looked grey in the distance, and as we came closer we could smell the sewage processor which squatted in the next bay behind the new pines. The sea came in frothy and brown across the sands, and left a thick layer of grime, shedding a filthy skin.

The air was thick too, of city shit. And cans from unenviable picnickers clattered up and down the sand, dragging up dust, playing with, tangled in, the ghosts of plastic bags.

We wrote our names, self-consciously, not knowing what else to do. Aki was embarrassed at having brought me here, but as we reclaimed a small patch of land we stirred some beach-spirit and drew the waves of zen temple gardens over our names, before stroking the sands flat again.

There were no shells, but a jelly fish had been beached here and Aki called me to it.

'Do you know the Japanese story about the jelly fish?'

I crouched beside her to listen. She was drawing patterns around the creature, drawing a sea with her hands, very gently.

'A sea dragon princess was once very ill, and was sure she would die, but she was told she would survive if she ate the liver of a live monkey. A jelly fish was given the task of going to land, finding a monkey, and bringing it back alive, and this it set out to do. As soon as it came into shore and pulled itself up on to the sand, a monkey came running up and introduced itself.

'"I like talking to things from the sea," it confided. "Some of my best friends are sea creatures you know."

' "Really?" grinned the jelly fish. "Well, if you like I could take you to visit the Princess of the Sea herself."

'The monkey leapt up and down with excitement and was happy to climb on the jelly fish's back, and the two set off across the waves. After a while the jelly fish, just to make quite sure, asked, "Monkey? Do have your liver with you?"

'The monkey felt a bit uncomfortable, and said, "Of course! But that's rather an odd question. Why do you ask?" And the jelly fish was so happy to have fulfilled its task so quickly that it began to chat about the Princess's illness.

'The monkey shifted and went a little green. The jelly fish noticed her discomfort and turned to ask if she was feeling seasick.

' "No," said the monkey, "but you should have told me this before. I have plenty of spare livers hanging on the trees in my home and I would have brought them all for the Princess of the Sea."

'So the jelly fish turned back to land, and this time, of course, the monkey could not be persuaded to visit the kingdom under the sea. The poor fish cried and wrung its hands – for jelly fish had hands then – but the monkey sat in her tree and laughed.

'When the jelly fish got home, everyone was so disappointed and angry that they beat it until it became like jelly, and all its descendants have been this way ever since. Also, they can no longer travel between land and sea as once they could.'

We sat silent, watching the dead creature. The beer and pocari sweat cans rattled along the shore, part of the sea's music now, pitiful but not ugly.

'My grandfather used to tell the same story to my mother when she was little, and it always made him laugh remembering how she had blamed the Princess. I can picture her standing on the beach, shouting out towards America, 'You are just a coward Princess stamping on things smaller than you.'

The wind was rising rapidly, and the dirty foam flecked our faces so that we were forced to taste the sewage. We turned from the sea and made our way back, fighting the wind with our heads down and our minds concentrating only on keeping to the narrow paths.

Aki's husband left his golf clubs, huge in their long bag, across the hallway. He shouted to the children to be careful as they ran about, but as they buried their faces in his side, he kissed the tops of their heads.

'Bedtime.'

'But we're going to watch the *stars*,' Atsuko sang the words so they rose up and down, and her head swayed to the rhythm.

'We're going to the stars,' her brother mimicked half-heartedly. 'The stars, the stars . . . ' and then, awakening, becoming serious, he demanded, 'Where's my stone?'

'What stone?'

'The stone Mummy got me from the sea?'

'Which stone was that?'

'The stone Mummy got me.'

'What does it look like?'

He seemed to think for a while.

'Small.'

'How small?'

He cupped his hands and looked down into them as if he was holding a breakable thing. He frowned in concentration, and then, satisfied with the picture in his mind, he held his hands out to his father.

'Like this.'

'Aki?' the father called. 'Where's Ichi's stone?'

'Which one?' She was still in the kitchen.

'How many are there?'

Atsuko watched, surprised at how easily her parents were responding to her brother's procrastination. I watched. The little boy grew bored and waddled toward me like a careful duck, asking something which I could not understand, shaking his head mournfully at my guessing.

155

'He's got hundreds. There's a box of them by the television, and some in the car.'

Slowly, Jun rose, and stood in front of the television while he bent over to pick up the box. Grandfather took another sip of his tea, patiently, waiting for his son to get out of the way.

'Are any of these okay?' Ichiro searched through the box carefully, picking up several, turning them round and round in his palms. Finally he shook his head. I laughed. His father had given up.

'Bedtime,' he repeated crossly.

'Mum*my*!' shrieked Ichiro, throwing the box of unwanted rocks to the floor. 'I want my *stone*.'

'Jesus Christ,' she muttered in English as she passed me.

I went into the kitchen and finished the washing-up. Grandfather looked up from the television and called over his shoulder, 'You are a guest, you shouldn't be doing that – where is Grandmother?' 'She's gone to the shop,' I said, and he snorted.

He unpacked his video camera and began connecting the wires together, muttering over the instructions. The next day we would all make a film 'In Memory of Internationalisation', to see how well the camera worked. Mimicking the Sony advertising campaign many students could now say to me in English, 'it's *passport* sized'. Now Grandfather was saying it too, and he had been persuaded to buy one of his own.

Outside the window Jun was repeating, as calmly as he could, 'But won't this one *do*? We can't go on searching all night.'

Aki came in from the car with the stone, and asked if Grandfather had taken his bath yet. He had. Now the children could have a turn, then me – always the same order, and everyone in the family got Grandfather's flaky skin. Only after the first time it didn't seem odd any more. Later, I went into Aki's room where she slept with Jun and her children on one big futon. She had sent me to go and look at the stone circle constructed beside Ichiro's head.

There was a very pleasant surprise awaiting, Moriya sensei informed me after a class one morning. There was to be a production of a most excellent play, performed at the town hall, and he had succeeded in buying three very much sought after tickets.

'My wife will come,' he said puritanically.

'And what is the play?'

'By your great Shakespeare.' He drew the tickets from his wallet and flourished them before my face. 'It is *King Lear*. Although I am sorry to say it is all Japanese actors, I am afraid. It will be strange for you, I think. You will have to – how do you say – see it feelingly.'

'And seeingly.'

'You know that woman has been called the gentler sex?' he asked after a while.

'Yes?' I smiled wearily.

'I do not agree with it.'

'Good,' I said.

He laughed a little, gallant laugh. 'Of course I think *you* are gentle,' he said. 'But many women these days are not.'

'Really?' I did not even look up but went on ticking and crossing papers. I could follow his thinking so clearly, it was as if he was talking in my head even when he was silent.

'Anna san? We must arrange where to meet now. The town hall is not so easy to find. Anna chan? How about meeting in Mitsukoshi fruit bar? We have not been there for some time. How about it?'

Before the curtain went up we took it in turns to photograph each other. Moriya sensei was dressed in the tail suit he had worn the day I was presented to the school, and both Mrs Moriya and I wore long black coats – we must have looked like a

157

family of vampires, we were all so pale and serious. The tension on stage as the curtain rose was no match for ours. We sat neatly in a row, watching the bloody mess before us.

We were sitting by the river again, though it was cold and unpleasant. The classrooms were even gloomier, and the wet dripped down the walls inside as well as out.

We were not always so serious. The week before we had sat round the boiler playing Monopoly for three hours, and somehow lost the little silver hat. Everyone tried for hotels on Park Lane and Mayfair these days, and it got quite rough – but I don't remember anything particularly special except Hiro's small voice of calm reminding us it was only a game.

But this day by the river we had just heard that a Japanese-Korean High School baseball team had for the first time been granted permission to play in the National League, so we were trying to discuss intolerance.

And the movement of peoples, peace, invasion, responsibility for the past and the like.

The text books had done their job well, and everyone told me that Japan was put upon by the rest of the world, though when pressed they conceded that Korea might be an exception. I didn't know enough myself to continue any sensible discussion, but told them instead of Olivier's film about Lady Hamilton, in which there is a wonderful sympathetic speech for poor old put-upon, valiant little England.

Then Miyo told us her grandmother was Korean. She watched Kazuo carefully as she spoke and seemed relieved once she had said it, but for once she didn't want to say anything more.

Six foreigners marched through a little street, the men much too big, the women too loud, but these days it did not matter because even a small town like this had three foreign teachers living in it – and another four schools had applied for and would probably be sent their own individual foreigner the following year . . . 'They *expect* us to be crass,' James told us. 'That's part of our appeal, our charm. We shouldn't *humour* them.'

'It is no more traditional than Hokkaido's festival,' Aki had said, 'it's just the kind of thing Lafcadio Hearn would have had ecstasies over, just his style. Of Japanese sentimentality.'

'Why so negative?'

'Oh, don't take any notice – it's beautiful really.'

I had accepted an invitation to go up to Yokote with James and Christobel to see the snow festival and to stay with one of James's college friends.

We turned up in the afternoon and sat on the floor in front of the electric heater in Tim-from-New-York's-apartment. All Tim wanted to see was the temple-storming, and that wasn't until the next day.

'I want to see the huge prick,' he repeated for the fourth or fifth time. 'They're going to storm the temple with this massive prick.'

'Why?' It was the first thing I had said, and everyone turned round as if surprised that I could speak. Tim smiled in the same kind, despairing way that sports teachers once smiled.

'Oh, some fertility rite I guess.'

I held my hands out to the electric heater and felt the blood throb into them, warming to the odd little world we were forming – the relief of an expatriate weekend.

Christobel said, 'One of my students is teaching me to play the flute.'

'I'd love to play the flute.'

'It's a pity we don't live nearer each other or you could come along too.'

We sat around drinking beer and telling stories about the times we had been forced to sing 'Yesterday' in front of a hundred people, or perform tea ceremony in front of a thousand . . . When the conversation came round to telephones with video screens I told everyone about the wonderful robot I had seen once, and my story went down much better with foreigners than it had done with the Japanese teachers. Nobody else had talked to a robot. Then Tim and Brian began to discuss baseball and Laura wanted to tell Christobel about her boyfriend back home who was a lawyer. James offered to show me the photographs of his trip to Nagasaki with Sayoko. The one I liked best was of a piece of ground with plants, a bit of red earth, and some crumbly tarmac, a sort of 'Three Ages of Earth', a compact version of what Mr Moriya's ex-forest had been through over the past year, even if it *would*, as he said, always be a forest at heart. At the front of the picture was a little sign which read in Japanese, then English, 'This is the earliest known asphalt path in Japan'.

'I though that was so typical,' said James, shaking his head affectionately. 'And you know they had escalators *outside*, so you didn't have to walk up the garden. And Verdi boomed all over the bay – because they figured Madame Butterfly lived there. They're rather sentimental about poor Butterfly.' He laughed. 'Probably the most tactless place I could have chosen to take Sayoko.'

I said I thought it probably was.

My hands were burning nicely against the radiator.

The six of us strode along the street, wet black snow slush sucking at our soles. At the first snow house we came to, we all trooped in and sat holding cups of hot *sake* and eating rice cakes. The poor little children whose father had beckoned us over did not know what had hit them – six huge foreigners making a progress through their pretty new home, eating them out of supplies when the evening had hardly begun.

'Perhaps we should go in separately next time,' said Christobel as we filed out into the cold again.

Down the main street of the old town each home had a domed snow house by its door, and children dressed in bright padded jackets and woollen hats served food to any visitors who came by. Some held exhibitions of objects floating in ice, ferns cut up to become the trees for tiny mountain scenes, and archetypal *ikebana* suspended for a while in complete stillness, petals untouched by our breath.

I took off my shoes at one threshold and bowed and apologised for intruding as I came in across the straw mats which lined the snow-floor. A shelf had been carved into the wall of the dome to store the food on, and a gas ring burned to heat the rice wine.

'Will you have some cakes?' A small child stepped forward. 'They are not very good, but please.'

'They are delicious.'

'I made them myself,' she said, watching me carefully. 'My granny told me how to make them and then I made them, see?'

It was warm inside the dome of snow, and bright, lit by gas flames and by candles pressed into the walls. The cushions were simply coloured, red, green, yellow and pink, and soft as I leant back – the hot wine coursed through me like blood.

'Would you like some sushi now?' the child said, taking my cup. 'And more *sake*?'

'Yes please.'

'We like having *you* here,' she giggled, digging her elbow into her brother. Her brother came forward then, and asked me very politely if I was a foreigner. She edged up behind him.

'Are you a foreigner?'

'No, I am Japanese,' I said softly. 'Don't I look Japanese?'

'Not really,' said the boy. Then he saw that I was smiling, and he knew, and he began to laugh a wheezy little laugh at himself and me. We both laughed. But the smaller child was troubled.

'Are you sure you are Japanese?' she whispered. She seemed to want to help me, an old person inside her would have taken my hand and told me, perhaps you are mistaken.

At the end of the street a hill rose toward the castle and up the hill hundreds of domes had been built each large enough to house a single candle, so the whole slope was alive with fire bound by ice. I asked a passer by what they meant – whether they were spirits? – but she laughed and said she did not know. 'But are they not pretty?' she said. *'Kirei-ne.'*

Aki said often that her husband had changed. He had grown to be what she called 'typical' – he played golf, he barked 'rice' and 'tea' like an officer when he wanted his bowl or cup filled – and one day, perhaps, he would become a 'wet dead leaf', difficult to sweep up, as his mother said of his father. I had seen the way Jun put his head down as he commanded her, as if he couldn't bear to see her face, but Aki said it was not as I imagined. He was just being lazy.

Going to Kyoto had been exceptional – I saw now that she would probably never have time like that without her children again, even the afternoon we cycled to the sea had been frowned upon.

Then one day in March I received a letter saying that she was in love with someone else – a teacher in her school, much older than she was. He was married, and his only child was at college already. She wrote that loving him was making her better able to love her husband, and that she had decided she would never leave her family, that it would not make her happy to do so.

She had told me about the summer she got back from America, when she and Jun had first met, when he wrote poetry and she wrote stories, and they had lived 'as Americans' in Kyushu, watching the sun fall off the far south of Japan every evening, and trying to stroke the wild horses that wandered in the nature reserves down there. They had stayed in a town which was always covered with volcanic ash, where the people walked about with umbrellas to keep themselves clean, and the huge volcano watched like a god from the other side of the estuary. One night Jun had crossed the water and slept at the volcano's foot amidst its own lunar landscape. He had said the lava made concrete and tarmac look ephemeral, and she had loved him for that (as one does, she chuckled).

*

'I never imagined what it would be like, really.'

A train slid in making the glasses and the plates chatter as the carriages entered directly above where we were sitting. Aki put her hand on the table, flat, and the quaking stopped.

'I never imagined how hard it would be, having a family – I never thought I would lose any sense of what I wanted and yet for a long while I did. I kept working because that seemed the only way to cling to my separateness – when I was with my family, with my parents-in-law, there was always cleaning and cooking and serving and I could not be myself, whatever that means. I think a lot of Japanese people who have been living in America or in Britain say this – that when they get back for a long while they don't feel *like themselves*, but with children it's even worse. And I did not feel good in my work either because I always thought I ought to be with my children, and I didn't know what I wanted. I only really began to see all this when I was pregnant again. It was the first decision that I had made for a long time. And I met you, and that reminded me of my time in America and of all the old things I used to feel strongly about. And soon after that I fell in love with Ono san. It all sort of came together.' She looked up at me and smiled. 'You probably think I'm crazy to stay with him, don't you?' But I did not.

'What do you think?' she asked, as another train passed northwards. 'What are you thinking?' I had actually been thinking how beautiful she looked, and how strong, but I did not say so. Because at the same time I felt wordless, in the way that one is sightless after opening one's eyes to the sun. As if her troubles were the troubles of more than the world. Nothing. Everything.

One day toward the end of term I was having tea with Mr Hayasaka and Watanabe sensei in the metal-working room when Mr Moriya came looking for me. An epitaph was troubling him, and he asked if I might explain the last line. He read it to us carefully.

> Deeply nestled in the earth
> This little child knew nothing –
> She died the moment of her birth
> And left her mother coughing.

'Perhaps she had whooping-cough?' he asked.

'Possibly,' I replied.

'People died of whooping-cough, in those days.'

'I don't know. Yes, I suppose they did.' I waited to see how he would get me back to my desk, but he was oddly silent. Hayasaka sensei offered him tea, and stiffly he sat down on the chair next to mine.

'It is nice and cosy in here,' he said to me. 'I understand why you like to visit here.' He pointed to a calendar on the wall, and added mysteriously, 'Anna sensei will be leaving us soon.'

'Not *soon*, I've got months to go,' I said, uneasy.

He looked coldly at me. 'But it seems as though you are half gone already.'

Steam from the kettle was rising behind him. It appeared to be coming from his ears.

'Do you think people really know nothing, at birth?' I asked politely, warily.

A procession of clowns, samurai and Swiss shepherdesses was in full swing – the figures spun round and round to tinny music above our heads. No one watched them, despite their lovely smiles and clean faces which someone must scrub each morning.

It was five o'clock. A mother was talking to a friend, and from the pushchair before her, her waking baby began to watch. The baby was only eight months old or so, had only lived in the town as long as me. Her head stretched backwards and her eyes rolled to try and catch the last of the figures as they disappeared and the castle doors clicked shut. Her arms rose up but she could not reach very far, and she let them sink again in disappointment. She seemed to wonder for a moment what to do. Then she started to yell, to kick, and her mother, bowing quickly to the friend, whisked her away through the legs of the crowd.

We met, the hard core of the English Speaking Society, for Kazuo's farewell, for he had a job to go to in Tokyo now that he had finished school. He had chosen a large company in the hope that they might put him through University one day.

From the clock we walked up Ichibancho towards Wagner's Café in silence, separated and brought together and separated again by other people, by groups of solid-legged girls in sailor suits swinging their bunched hair, by thin boys eating icecream sheepishly. Mainly there were young people about, the Salary-men and Office Ladies not yet released for the evening, the daytime shoppers already back home.

The groups of young people stood about, watching each other, giggling. Fingering, untucking their uniforms. Ruffling their hair.

In the café the walls were covered in European black and white photographs – the mournful pretty face of a gypsy child, a skinny girl in a petticoat walking through the lip of water between land and sea. I did not at all like the proprietor who had taken these pictures on his travels in Europe. He was tall and he wore casual jerseys and he could have been Italian as easily as Japanese.

'Well, *I* think he is very handsome,' said Miyo leaning toward me.

'You find everyone handsome,' Kazuo said, and her face punctured.

The Viennese coffee came with thick sticks of cinnamon to use for stirring in the cream, and I dropped mine in, letting it bore a hole through and rest in the dark coffee beneath, spreading its flavour. Kazuo said I was messy. Miyo licked the cream off her stick and watched us. Hiro, oblivious, ordered a second piece of chocolate fudge cake, then looked up at the photographs.

'I don't know if I like them or not,' he said thoughtfully.

We all tried harder to be cheery then. They began talking about a game show that I had not heard of, and they were amused that I had missed it, that my knowledge was so haphazard. I was amused too at first, but then as they began to throw names at me and to discover the depth of my ignorance the joke got tiresome.

'So – I can do the tea ceremony better than any of you.'

Miyo snorted.

'And you know how to tickle carp,' said Hiro. 'That might be useful one day.'

Kazuo gave me a box wrapped in blue paper, with the corners folded in perfectly like a new-born, creaseless thing, an archetype of a present. And a neat pink ribbon, furled in a bow at the top.

'You shouldn't have bought me a present.'

He nodded at me to open it, and the ribbon slipped off easily, it slipped through my knees to the floor in a long line with the crimped furls forming a head at one end.

We had not met outside school alone before, and the next day he would take the train down south to Tokyo, to the formal speeches welcoming him to his new company, to adult life.

There was a box inside, and then paper and then to my horror, a mirror.

He did not say anything silly though.

He just said that a mirror kept the spirit of its past owners, and that ordinary people could stay on earth that way.

'Do you remember the story of Mugenyama, in the text book? My grandmother had a similar experience during the war, she was very upset to give her mother's mirror to make weapons, but finally she did.'

We had read of Mugenyama in a lesson. Some priests had decided that they wanted a new bell and had asked all the local women to give up their metal mirrors so that they might be melted and refashioned. The woman in the story had given hers readily at first but then seeing it on a heap waiting to be destroyed in the temple she had felt terrible regret. She wanted it back, and she felt guilty that she wanted it. She wanted to see her mother and her mother's mother's mother one more time, and she regretted all the days she had looked in the mirror and seen only herself and not tried to see the spirits of her ancestors in its smooth deep surface.

I had not been happy reading this aloud.

For the woman's mirror had not melted. She was selfish, I read. The villagers taunted her, said her mirror was too hard to melt, as hard as her heart had become, and thus humiliated she had drowned herself. Only then was she granted respect. The mirror succumbed to the flames, and the priests got on with casting their bell.

I was getting angry remembering this story but I did not know what Kazuo thought of it. I wondered if my anger would have seemed pointless to him. I thought it would. It *was*. But then it was also important, one or the other, I couldn't tell.

'Thank you,' I remembered to say. He had understood my fear of disappearing, which he translated as a fear of death, and slowly I realised that the gift was a recognition of this. I gave him a glass paperweight with a twist of coral inside, which seemed an odd present too. A sea which he could hold in his hand, perhaps. Neutral. Value-free. Sea protected both our countries, unquestioningly.

I forgot the end of the Mugenyama tale, but later I reread it and felt my anger had been foolish, for the story could have been meant in any number of ways.

Before the woman died, she said that anyone who broke the bell through their ringing of it would be rich for ever. She knew how far neighbourly love would reach, knew that when people heard of her promise they would be flocking from miles around to try and destroy that bell. Up the ragged temple path the endless altered people came . . . And the valley resounded. And the locals were full of dismay. Farmers stuffed rags in their ears, and the priests had a hard time meditating.

So one day they gave in. The priests put the bell on a donkey cart, and they went crossly up into the mountains, the donkey snatching a bite to eat now and then. They arrived in a valley where they thought no people had ever been, and they lifted the bell down and rolled it over and over, until they reached a swamp. And they rolled it right into the swamp.

You can imagine the sucking sound as a huge bell sinks.

You can draw your own world of allusions, beginning with the melted faces of all those women. While the donkey trots back home up and down the hills and valleys, rid of her load.

At the top of the hill it was snowing, but we were so close to the snow clouds themselves that it was hard to tell for sure. The air was so dense. Someone said it was minus twenty, but I did not think it felt as cold as that, unless minuses were less easy to sense than pluses. We were being bustled together by Hayasaka sensei for a group photo. Not that we would be able to tell who was who, except the ones in fluorescent pink glitzy snow suits, who might want to have a picture for the snow suit's sake. Mine was white so I wouldn't show at all, which was good because I felt frightful in it.

Sasaki sensei, the young teacher who had been to London, was elected as my guide. It caused us all some excitement to have me and no Mr Moriya. Sasaki sensei spoke a bit of English and they seemed to think my Japanese would desert me up there in the mountains.

That morning I had been up and down the beginners' slope and I had enjoyed it. First I had done straight lines, solid as a descending angel in an early Renaissance painting. Then Yoshimoto sensei had shown me how to turn corners and zig-zag slowly by shifting the weight from one foot to the other, allowing a surprisingly easy elegance. In a few hours I was as good at it as everyone else on the slope, and could do it with my eyes closed. I could do it like a lullaby.

'So,' Hayasaka sensei had said over lunch, 'you'll come up with us this afternoon?'

'Up? Where to?' I said casually, hiding my mingling excitement and unease.

He said everyone was going to take the cable-car to the summit of the longest slope, and spend the afternoon coming down. He said it was not particularly steep, and there were wonderful views.

'I'm not sure I'm ready for it.' But I was tempted by the idea of the views, being British and brought up on Michelin guides too. I longed to drift through the snowy mountains as I had drifted down the baby slope, and I told myself it would be much the same sort of thing. 'Do you think I'm ready?'

It didn't take much to persuade me. I thought I had never picked up a sport half so quickly before. But when we got to the top we seemed very high up indeed.

I thought of Mr Moriya, who knew my weak spots now like the back of his pink hand. He had said, everyone will be good at skiing and they won't have much time to help you learn. He had said, they will all get unpleasantly drunk and Yoshimoto sensei will be the only woman there.

'You will have to pay. It's quite expensive I am sorry to say,' he had tried at last in desperation.

He could not forbid me to go.

Conversations like this spiralled out of control with us, and we would end up saying the most ludicrous things – I would say, but I've always wanted to ski, or, but why don't you come? and he would reply that skiing was a tedious sport, that there was nothing like walking, and wouldn't I prefer to spend a quiet weekend with him (and his wife of course)?

But I went all the same.

Sasaki sensei said he would stay by me until I felt ready to take the plunge. I was glad of his English, because it allowed me to put all my effort into concentrating on the five-mile slope ahead. We shuffled along to the starting point, and already my skis were locking together at the back and the front in turns, while my legs jellied.

Some of the others tipped over the edge and vanished.

'I thought it wasn't going to be steep?'

'Not much of it. Just first part, then flat after that,' Sasaki sensei said patiently.

The trees were covered in snow – not only on the branches, but all over, each tree was covered by a thick white dunce's cap. It was not like being on earth at all. We seemed unnaturally high up. Beyond our mountain top there was no view because we could not see through the air. Air, ground, trees, were reduced to snow, and we would be too if we stood about.

He asked how I liked the point of view.

Before us the slope descended and all the other teachers were soon barely visible dots near its base.

'You see, you can see the bottom of this first slope. It is not long.'

I knew if I walked I would still be on the mountain at nightfall among the bears. Also, I was ruining Sasaki sensei's trip.

We compromised. I held his waist and he skied in front of me. He called out 'Right!' and 'Left!' and I stood heavily on each foot accordingly, but it was clumsy and a muddle, not at all like the morning, and we fell on top of each other, skis tangled, almost before we had begun. Snow stuffed up our sleeves and down our necks. We seemed to be the last people left on this particular mountain.

Again we set off, me holding his waist tight, trying to let him control my moving, but when we turned a corner and headed straight down for a moment every muscle in me petrified and I pulled him leadenly to the snow.

'Yes, we will have to walk this part,' he said at last.

Relieved of the skis I chattered all the way down, saying things I'd never have mentioned to him in a different landscape – that I was so glad Mr Moriya had not come, and that since December I had felt more in control of myself, more relaxed. I said it was nice to get to know other teachers this weekend, and that I was sorry so many months had passed already.

(He was probably thinking, thank goodness.)

But he said politely that he thought it would be better now my Japanese had improved.

All the way down the mountain I talked, asking him how he liked teaching – asking about his trip to England. I remembered he had said something about liking the British Museum so we had a brief conversation about that, but it seemed very far away and irrelevant. As we walked lower the branches of trees were revealed, their dark arms no longer snowed under but touching one another at the sides of our path. The snow looked blue in the dusk, and once we saw paw prints leading away into the woods.

I did not believe that Moriya sensei had no power over me any more, but I was learning to talk myself away from him. It did not always work – often my words echoed hollowly and came circling back to me, to the knot in me – Moriya sensei and I. But sometimes not.

When we got near the foot of the mountain we put our skis back on, for the final slope was a gentle one. We glided down in silence, in the dark at first, but while we were descending floodlights for the evening skiers were suddenly illumined, making the snow white again – welcoming us.

Over drinks that evening the deputy headmaster stumbled up to me.

'Know any British ski champions?' he asked hopefully, as if he spoke to me every day, only it was the first time ever he had done so, for mostly he was fast asleep hunched over his desk.

I wished I could have continued the conversation, but knew no names at all.

'Tell me about some of the Japanese ones,' I smiled enthusiastically, and he sat down by me, and poured me *sake*.

'So, you can drink this can you! Very good, very good.' And then he said, 'Well, I never knew you understood Japanese.'

'Well, hardly,' I said with the right amount of modesty.

He talked on and on in a fudgy-drunken voice I could not understand, but even so I enjoyed being with him.

Spring

When the cherry blossom front finally reached us in the north, Aki asked me to come blossom-viewing with her family. For some days the flowers were all we thought about. In the newspaper I read of a zoo keeper who was trying to get the revellers banned from the park next to his zoo, because the noise was keeping the animals awake, and some were sick, and all were sleeping through the day so no visitors could see them. He wrote that in the past it had not been so bad, but because of the new portable karaoke machines the singing went on loud all through the night. And I had seen, at eight one morning, a respectably dressed business man curled up snoring under a tree, presumably overlooked by his companions as they shuffled off before dawn.

At school the blossoms reached the second floor classrooms.

Everyone seemed happy to be starting the new year in such a hopeful season.

Jun had bought a new dog which did not like me at all, but although I was happy to keep quiet and out of its way, he insisted that it came on our picnic, and that I learnt to reason with it.

'Show me.' I was suspicious, for I did not think it was a very reasonable kind of dog.

After we laid down our mat under the cherry trees, Jun said he would teach me some elementary dog psychology.

'I thought the English were good with dogs,' he muttered. 'But you are not good with dogs at all.'

'I'm good with cats,' I said humbly, but clearly that was beside the point.

The dog was put on a lead, and I was told to perambulate the four edges of the mat. The first lap I ran with its devil's breath fiery against my heels.

'Now pat him,' said Grandfather, hands on his hips, for they were all standing around watching the spectacle.

'I quite want to keep my fingers on,' I tried to joke, tried to cling to what was left of my sense of humour. I was concerned by the froth around its lips.

'It will be fine,' they all chorused like angels. The dog snarled nastily, and lifted one side of its lip to reveal yellow fangs as my feeble hand approached. Its skull throbbed hot, and I could feel a growling buzz like a hornet's nest in its head – but as I stroked the buzzing subsided.

'You see.'

It was a triumph of dog psychology, and I had to believe it, for the rest of the evening the creature was up on my knees smothering me in yellowing saliva kisses.

The sky was still blue long after it seemed dark under the trees, and the lanterns looped from branch to branch, pinkish in the half light, and the flowers were soft as the Andrex ads back home. Everything got blurry. The air was warm but the colours cool, the opposite exactly of the maple leaves. The *sake* barely tasted, but went on slipping through us until even Grandmother was singing a sentimental love song about regret and a woman in white that was oh so many years ago, along with a family on the mat next to us, who had a portable karaoke just like the kind Grandfather wanted.

I was just conscious enough to remind Jun that he shouldn't be driving us home, but he did all the same. We got there, singing still. I dragged futons to the guest room – the *tatami* room – and spread them beneath the shrine, watched over by a sweet smiling old couple dressed in formal *kimono* from earlier this century.

Before I was quite awake, I felt eyes on me, and when I wakened fully I saw the wretched little dog staring with love into my face. Its tail began thumping against the *tatami*, and it leapt forward with a smile of joy.

Jun had recently got back from a business trip to Thailand and Singapore and he showed us photographs – him and colleagues sipping cocktails in the wicker chairs of Raffles Hotel – him and colleagues posing in front of a fancy temple.

'They don't get any work done,' said Aki, 'but they keep the tourist industry going, that's for sure.'

He had bought me as an *omiage* a scarf – a thick Thai silk with turquoise rim and huge flowers woven in every possible blue. I tried to tell him about something my mother always said – when I had asked her, ceaselessly, what is your favourite colour? – because that kind of thing seems so important when you first realise other people have different favourites. My father's was yellow. People at school had favourites, people's mothers had favourites too. But always my mother's answer was unsatisfactory for she would say, 'There are too many different colours in each colour – how can I say?' Or sometimes to my exasperation, 'What do you mean?' And I so wanted to pin her down.

'There are enough colours in this to need no other colours but blue,' I said clumsily.

As usual, the whole family roared with laughter when I asked if I could sit in the garden and read for a while, as the sun was out. Only Mr Moriya understood that strange English masochistic desire.

Aki told me over the telephone about a new teacher in her school, who, when he heard she had been to America, said, 'Is it true that the taxi drivers are all thieves over there?'

He wanted to go on honeymoon to New York, but he had got cold feet because of what he had heard, especially about taxis. Aki told him about the Japanese driver who had cheated me once by going a route three times longer than was strictly necessary, and he was terribly shocked and sent his apologies to me. He was also going on a weekend class to learn how to behave abroad, how to cope with the day to day trauma, because his bride to be had been to Hong Kong and LA and Paris, and he was afraid of looking silly in front of her. He wanted to be quite sure who to hand his passport to and things like that.

The Table Manners class was on the ninth floor, the hotel porter told me with a respectful bow.

'You are an English teacher at the school?' Yes, I said. How nice, he sighed, to have foreign teachers in schools. To learn real English. Yes, indeed. Internationalisation. I envy young people these days. He came and stood close by me as we waited for the lift, and I thought he would follow me in, but he just stood there waving and bowing until the doors cut between us.

I glided upward, and the sweet electric voice sang at each floor, 'ni-kai desu, san-kai desu'. There was no fourth floor because the word for four was the same as the word for death. And no one would want to say, 'death, please'. On the ninth, the carpets were cheap but smooth under foot – the chandeliers plastic, made of tiny cubes of light.

Kazuo had written to me about the lights he worked under in the Toyota laboratory, the glaring cold flat light which throbbed like acid through his head and made him white inside, white and dead empty, at the end of each day. His whole letter was about the light.

All the tables were draped in heavy white sheets, and there was a bowl of roses in the centre of each, then candle sticks on either side.

'This fork,' Yoshimoto sensei was saying, 'is for fish, and this knife is for fish also.'

'Aren't they pretty,' murmured the girl I was placed next to.

'This glass is for the wine that you drink *during* the meal, and this is for the *sweet* wine that we have afterwards.'

We stood with our hands on the back of our chairs, while Yoshimoto sensei introduced us to some more of the objects arranged before us. There was a low-sided bowl, then a plate, and then a slightly larger plate underneath that, and we were told to observe the flower-like effect of the arrangement.

'Europeans do not mix colours as we do on special occasions. Often they use simple white dishes like these – they are called,' she said in English, '*fine china* or *bone china*.' The girl beside me ran her finger around the edge of the bowl, and then along the silver knife next to the fish knife.

'Now here,' Yoshimoto sensei said, 'is the serviette. You can fold it like this, in a peak, or for a party you could fold it into a fan.'

'Do you have fans in Europe?' Noriko, who was sitting on the other side of the roses, whispered, and I nodded. I knew Noriko because she was one of the few new first years to join the English Speaking Society.

The manager of the hotel catering section appeared and apologised for being late. He adjusted the microphone to make it higher although if anything Yoshimoto sensei was the taller of the two.

'On behalf of the staff at the Imperial Hotel, I welcome you all to this year's Table Manners Banquet. It is a great pleasure for us to be hosts to the Technical High School yet again, and I hope that this lesson will be remembered with affection for many years to come and that such experiences will be seen as furthering the interests of world peace as we try hard to include an international approach in all our actions. Bon appetit.' That was the gist of it anyway. But while he spoke I noticed that one of the roses had a very tiny caterpillar trying to cross from a petal on the outside to one further inside, only it couldn't quite reach. It would stretch as full as its segments could go and then, just as it was about to touch the other side of the gulf – giddy, I supposed – it would contract, sharply, all the air punched out, folded in on its despair.

'Anna sensei?'

I refocused on the spread of the table, to the room, and saw Yoshimoto sensei smiling purposefully at me. The English *itadakimasu* – for a moment I could think of nothing whatsoever to say. Clumsily I launched into an old grace I had once recited to myself, when I was twelve and frantic for something to believe in despite my unholy family – because of them. *For what we are about to receive may the Lord make us truly thankful.*

The chairs were rattling before I had finished.

*

Noriko was an expert in Table Manners because her older sister studied western cookery and etiquette at college. She showed our group how to rest the spoon between finger and thumb like a fountain pen and draw it backwards and forwards through the soup, raising it up and over the bowl in a semi-circle to our lips. The spoon should do a water mill movement, rather than a piston-like backwards and forwards. Everybody watched. Then we began to make our own circles, seriously, frowning until we got in the swing of it, and I thought, they are so careful, so sweet, such small things fascinate them – forgetting the cater-pillar – and then I noticed one or two of them exchanging wicked glances, speeding up, going so fast that little droplets of orange flew off and seeped out flat and matt on the white table cloth.

'If you don't want more wine,' Yoshimoto sensei was perhaps concerned with the giggling, 'you can place your hand gently across the top of the glass, like so. And always place your spoon to the right, pointing out to your right hand side, of course – and remember to do that for the knives and forks also. The spoon and fork should always curve upwards, and the sharp edge of the knife should always be on the left, as they have been laid here.' I had forgotten that I knew anything practical like this, and it was pleasant to remember that I too knew something of etiquette, having been the clumsy one for months now. I even recalled faintly that cutlery should be left at four o'clock on the plate, but I didn't bother to say this as all those around me had the wrong type of watch, so I would only have confused things.

The eating began to get tedious. After skinning the fish and picking the bits of flesh from the fine bones, I sat and watched everyone elbow into steak and sautéed potatoes. Every few minutes Yoshimoto sensei stood up and told us something, and sometimes I knew it and sometimes I did not, but I made myself feel good both ways – I should not know *too* much about this sort of thing.

'Why aren't you eating the meat?' Noriko asked me.

'Because I'm vegetarian.' This normally shut people up, or else drew forth a soft understanding clicking sound. But Nori-ko's father was a business man who went to America. She was tough.

'But you eat fish?'

'Only because I have to here or I'd starve.' She did not look at all convinced, and neither was I.

'Would you eat whale meat then?' I told her it was a good question, biding time, because no, of course I would not eat whale meat. No. No, I said.

'Why?'

The dreamy girl next to me was impressed by Noriko's attack, and I could see she had paused, smiling up from her steak.

'You know,' Noriko continued, 'that it was the Americans who first introduced whaling to Japan, yet now they blame us.'

I had visited an old whaling port once and the buildings still echoed with the pain of the past, pain that lingered as if its throbbing could not disperse because it was not wanted elsewhere. Thick iron coils and pulleys were starting to rust, and lay about indolent like fat old men who have had what they wanted all their lives and might just get away with never feeling humiliation. The brickwork crumbled as I ran my hands along the wall, and the air I stirred up smelt deathly. But then again, the grass grew greener round about for all that blood which had fallen.

I could hear James laughing at my sloppy thinking.

I could play back in my mind the video I once saw of a whale with huge harpoons driven thick again and again into its flesh, and the flesh ripping open – the blood filling the sea and stretching outwards like blood stretching into a wide blister under the skin. And the terrible dark eyes of the whale. And the screaming. Over the hills of England too, I heard pigs in a well-placed, out-of-the-way sort of corrugated grey slaughter house, screaming, turning the sun cold.

And worse things had been done, that was for sure.

'What's the difference between killing a whale and killing a cow?' Noriko asked, and I said that I didn't know, but wasn't killing a helpless prawn worst of all because it was so difficult to conceive its suffering, and so many needed to die, but oh, weren't they so good to eat? Cut down their middles and flattened onto rice. Deep fried and floating on a bowl of *soba* noodles.

'Sea food risotto,' giggled the girl beside me, picking up her knife and fork and carefully continuing with her beef. 'Sea food risotto at Benito's next to the station is very tasty and good.' I think it was the longest sentence in English she had ever said.

'In New York airport's duty free,' said Noriko, 'they sell as a souvenir "Original Texan teriyaki-flavoured beef". My father brought us back some, and it was *delicious*.'

We sat in front of two large jam jars. One contained gravel and some chunks of rather uncouth looking grey rock, the other contained pieces that were grey and brown, some both grey and brown. One was marked 'Souvenir from Mont Blanc' and the other 'Souvenir from Mount Snowdon'.

'The French were not as friendly as the English.'

'Welsh.'

'Oh,' he giggled. 'You are so right to correct me.'

'Were the Welsh friendly then?' I leant back and smiled inanely at the stones, then I told him the joke about if Wales were flattened out it would be bigger than England, and watched it fall about as flat as the Sahara. I knew there must be a reason for the appearance of these rocks this evening, so I waited, I folded my arms, to see what he would come up with.

'I have a very interesting plan,' he said at last. 'Now that winter is over, I would like to take you to Mount Zao to collect stones as a souvenir of your time in Japan.' I thought it rather premature to be thinking of souvenirs, but was relieved that the plan did not involve too great an obstacle. At least it wasn't Mount Fuji. Zao was surprisingly unambitious – even somewhere I had wanted to go to myself. He seemed pleased that I agreed so readily, and said with a generous sweep of the hand,

'You could bring Christobel too, if you wish.'

Now that's an idea, I thought.

He had seen a photograph of Christobel taken in Yokote and seemed keen to meet her.

'She sounds like she is not quite a typical Australian, is that so?'

'Really, I could not say.'

'Perhaps she has something of an English sensibility?' he asked hopefully.

Christobel was proclaimed second daughter before we had crossed the threshold, and I felt like reminding them she wasn't even English, so confused was I to see that it might not have been me all the fuss was about. Mrs Moriya loved her red hair and fiddled with it, and said how pretty it was. She had never said anything like that to me.

I had suspected she didn't like my effect on Mr Moriya, but now I began to think it was me she'd felt dubious about – after all she knew, I'm sure, the strange mixture of feelings surrounding my relationship with her husband. She was probably the one person whom I could have discussed it with, but how could I have initiated such a conversation?

The deerstalker was coming, and it seemed like an old friend I hadn't seen for months.

He had put a Tyrol feather in it.

And he wore German breeches, and thick long socks, and walking boots waited in the porch like the kind you meet five miles up a hill in the middle of the Lake District, or on the President of the Ramblers' Association.

'Are these clothes alright?' I asked, holding my arms out and looking down at my feet.

'Yes,' he looked me up and down. 'It will do.'

Christobel did most of the talking. She complimented the books and the bagpipes, and sat at the piano stool, running her fingers over the keys. I don't think I had ever delighted them as much as she did. After my initial discomfort, I was grinning silently like the happy fish that got away.

We waved goodbye to Mrs Moriya (who knew something we did not) and set off down the garden path, briskly of course, passing in file under the arch with the 'Home Sweet Home' sign and beneath that the *kanji* of Mr Moriya's pen name – rather his 'nom de plume' – which he had chosen many years before but had not yet had the opportunity to use, as he had decided to put the epitaphs under his own name.

He pointed out the tarmac where the forest had been – the last stage, the painting of the white lines for the cars to sit between, would be completed in the next few weeks. Christobel was sympathetic and said how sad he must be to lose something so beautiful under tarmac, and he told her, yes, but after all a forest was always a forest at heart and it would never be truly destroyed. I thought it looked pretty close to being truly destroyed, but rather than say anything I tried to think of some clever connection to make between this and his gravestone enthusiasms – and then I realised how happy I was just to dream off. On the bus I leant back and watched the swish of the road passing under the wheels, and didn't try to keep up with their talking.

But by the time we got to the foot of Zao I could tell Christobel was flagging somewhat.

She had not paced herself as I had, being inexperienced in excursions such as these.

As we got off the bus she whispered to me, 'It's like going for a day's outing with a whirlwind.'

At last, at last! I wanted to sing – at last it has been seen.

'Full speed ahead!' he said, raising the deerstalker. '*Gambatte ne* – try hard – good luck!'

It was not the stroll he had made it out to be. At first we walked along a path which had been well strewn with picnic litter, but he told us not to worry as we'd soon be off the beaten track.

'The landscape will remind you of Wordsworth.' He flashed me a knowing smile, and turned to Christobel. 'Do you know Wordsworth?'

'Indeed I do,' said Christobel resolutely.

'So you study him in Australia, do you?'

Once we began the ascent he was off like a rocket.

'I hope I'm like this when I'm sixty,' Christobel panted. I think that was the last nice thing she said about him because for a while after that we used all our breath to keep up. And an hour and a half later we were very fed up indeed.

We came to a rock face. Christobel saw it before I did and said she wasn't going up.

Really, it was very steep, with rocks which crumbled when we touched them.

In general I would have said that I liked climbing about on rocks. Once I had a whole flock of invisible mountain goats I used to play with instead of other children and when I went to the beach I'd get them to clamber about with me rather than play on the sand. But no self-respecting mountain goat would have climbed this. I said I wouldn't go up either.

We stood stubborn as donkeys and waited for him to come up with a suggestion.

Which of course he did.

At one side of the rock face there was a hole through which we could climb. He went up first to reconnoitre and after some time reappeared and said all was well, although his face was a shade redder than usual.

'Watch your step carefully,' he said beamingly to Christobel, and she replied with teeth clenched that she believed she was doing so.

He held out his hand to me and I thought, you might have learnt not to do that by now. I was glad that Christobel for the present seemed even less tolerant than me.

We struggled on, clutching at stones and bunches of grass, and sometimes they held and sometimes we slipped back. At one point the rock arched right over us and we were in a tunnel – we could see the light at both ends easily, but Mr Moriya's spirit of adventure was aroused and he produced a torch, shining it back into our faces, making us wince in turn.

'I don't think that's necessary,' said Christobel, in a gravelly voice which thrilled me.

'We're nearly there.' He sounded like he was grinning.

'We'd damn well better be,' said Christobel not too quietly.

But we were nowhere near the top. When we came out onto the path again above the rock face, it looked like we had as far to go as we had come, and then I began to feel I shouldn't have involved Christobel in this. I should have known exactly how it would turn out, and I felt like a child who has encouraged a friend to come on an outing with a difficult relation, and halfway through realises that it would have been easier to cope numbly alone.

'Nice view,' he said. 'Is it not?'

And then he said, overlooking our crossed eyebrows,

'I've brought the jam jar, by the way. For the stones. And one for Christobel too. We must remember to fill them when we get to the summit.'

'If we get there,' I laughed, but my heart was not in it.

Once, I glanced behind me and saw the mountain range lumbering away into the distance, oblivious to our pain, and the trees were just beginning to send out new pale leaves, welcoming the equally pale and tentative sun.

It was lucky it wasn't hotter.

'At least the temperature is exactly right for this,' I called up, but neither of them answered – Mr Moriya was probably too far ahead.

'I'm *so* sorry,' I said to Christobel as I came alongside her, and she returned a wan unblaming smile.

'Can't you wait for a bit!' I heard someone yell, and then with a falling feeling realised it was me. He turned round.

'Are you *tired*?' he asked with a devilish smile.

I had absolutely no idea what was going through his head, but if he wanted to prove that a fifty-eight-year-old man was stronger than two women in their twenties put together, then that was fine – for all we cared – he could believe it.

And yet it wasn't that.

He was in his element, I suppose. He was alone before us – leading but alone – and marching up towards the sky. He was European in dress, Japanese in sensibility – he was a teacher who would rather have spent his life reading poetry and writing novels, and who made do with translating words from the dead. He found the epitaphs very funny. I always forgot that, pitiless in my selection. Ah, the cruelty of youth, he might have said – for even that he wanted. But I had had enough of being thought young. That was why the English Speaking Society kept me sane, I supposed, and why a part of me loved Kazuo.

Moriya sensei found the epitaphs funny. They were his way of laughing at death.

But he was scared of living too. And now he was performing for us, lost in his great game, now and again spurred on by the thought of his captive audience, whose admiration he so desired. He thought he had it today. He was quite un-aware that the audience had slipped away already. He was like a child, very like a child, and my heart was reaching out to him.

Was that all he asked?

When we got to the top everything slotted back into sensible perspective immediately. The sun lit the valley we had begun in and it looked much prettier from above than it had from within, as ugly parts of the earth must look from outer space. We had not heard the birds before either, deafened by our own noisy throbbing thoughts, but now it seemed as if the mountains for miles were riddled with them, they were jumping up all over the place like singing fleas.

Down the other side of the ridge, below us, was the old crater – now filled with green water and glittering like a live eye, a moody eye because it changed colour – from pink to grey to blue to green, depending on the season. I asked Mr Moriya if the volcano was dead, and he said, no, it was dormant.

We all agreed it was an exceptionally lovely lake.

We sat down and drank our coffee and ate rice balls filled with salmon, and then we each had one with a pickled plum. When I bent down to hide my plum under the stones, I remembered the jam jar, but did not say anything because I wanted to see when he would remember. Only I forgot again, and after some time we began to descend.

Ten minutes down Christobel turned to me and said in a rushed whisper, 'Quick, pick up some stones and say they came from the top, or we'll have to go back up again.'

I was impressed.

We filled our pockets with a variety, bending our knees as we continued to walk, swooping down, scooping up a handful, up, pocket, down. When he looked round we straightened our backs and froze like we were playing musical statues.

Our feet just wandered on with no effort now, and before us we could see the mountains.

'Oh no,' he said, turning. 'We had better go back. You know what we have forgotten?'

At first he seemed slightly suspicious – he eyed us carefully, asked if they were actually from the summit.

'Yes,' said Christobel, looking straight into his eyes, something I could never do.

'Ah, very good, very good, you both understand my meaning,' he sighed, and his words clearly signified much to him. 'You understand the delicacy of this. It is a very nice thing to have such a memory.' He nodded to himself and we all set off again, listening to the crunch of free stones at our feet, watching them leap up from our toes.

'I keep getting images of fleas,' I said to Christobel conversationally, and we suggested reasons why that might be but none seemed very satisfactory.

Later still we came to a green valley, a grassy valley, more like England than anything I'd seen in Japan. And there was a European kind of river running through – a bog-simple, rather muddy river with rough grassy banks.

We crossed and recrossed it, singing, and I taught Christobel the Irish song,

> Oh it's a nice place to be
> o-on a fine summer's day
> watching all – the wild flowers
> that ne-er-er do decay . . .

Mr Moriya was happy too. He even clapped his hands to the Celtic rhythm, and said, 'Ahh.'

For a moment I felt tempted to put my arm around him, to protect him.

Back in my room, Christobel got me to dance in front of the mirror. She held my hands and angeled them up and down like Laura Ingalls Wilder in the snow. She shook my shoulders, and hugged me, and then I realised how long it was since I had been hugged. I held her too.

'Thank you for coming. It made such a difference.'

'It's fine.'

We twisted and clapped, and moved our arms so slowly we couldn't see the moving, and then we spun round and round until we fell all over the matted floor.

I read about a Tokyo business man who bought Van Gogh and Renoir paintings only to store them in bank vaults. He was proud to say he had only glanced at each once, to confirm that they were his and his alone, before locking them away. He seemed to see it as a form of self-control, a sort of super-fine aestheticism.

In the newspapers at the same time was the story of the sixty-nine-year-old woman who had been convicted for murder in the United States, and sentenced to death. Her picture was every-where. Miyo kept asking me if it would really be carried out, and all I could repeat was that I did not know. It did not fit her idea of America.

Miyo was quieter these days, and it was Noriko who laughed and joked and talked of emigrating. Miyo had a job more or less lined up with a firm which designed vacuum cleaners, not to design, but to make tea and answer the telephone at first, then more might come of it.

In Disneyland you can ride like Wordsworth's Peter or Chibi Maruko chan in a dream boat. You sail round a corner, and through that immortal Kensington nursery where the doll's house maids wave, and the tin soldiers salute you. The curtains draw back and the window flings open, and nervous people scream here – because outside there is nothing holding you. The floor is gone, and the hull of the boat swings in the night – you do not see at first, it takes time to reason, that what you thought was supported from below is actually held from the unseeable ceiling above. Like with Superman, you cannot see the wires. (My sister when she was very small said – Of course he's not *really* flying, they've got him on strings to the clouds.)

Beneath the boat lights appear, and the moving lights of pin prick cars, roving, show where the roads are, and there is a serpent shape with no light at all, winding thick through the centre. Then you notice Big Ben – and understand that the eyeless serpent is the Thames, all tiny beneath as you sail over.

I dreamt of going hom, tipping the boat a little.

Aki was talking about her feelings for Ono sensei, while we walked between flowers displayed for a newly invented iris festival, somewhere on the very edge of the city. She talked about his theories of desire, and of greed in modern Japanese society – about the lack of direction and belief – all the big things. She was breaking down his ideas and rebuilding them herself, then I would take them from her and do the same for me, like – was it DNA in biology classes? – breaking, selecting, reusing, understanding.

She called to the children and the four of us held hands to climb up the slope overlooking the iris garden.

An old woman wearing traditional bulky country clothes stepped heavily over one of the irrigation canals and began to make her way with determination through the iris stalks, pushing them firmly to left and right.

We watched.

She stopped right at the centre of the display and looked about her. Perhaps from the ground she was shorter than the irises and could not be seen, but I suppose she did not care either way. Bunching up her clothes she crouched down – a flash of naked skin – and she was up again and off like a warrior through to the other side.

She cut beautifully, this old woman, through Moriya sensei's vision.

I wondered what she feared, but could not even begin.

And what had I feared. Becoming invisible through too much moving. And through having no direction, and no one single goal, for always until now the pattern had been – institution, holiday, institution, holiday – combined sometimes, but never neither. I had feared my ability to melt into other people's fantasies, finding a frame in them.

But now?

Moriya sensei was much older than me, but in some respects his fears had seemed similar to my own. He thought at one time he might become more real through me. He clung to ghostly references which failed him. He trusted in the wrong places.

Though I could never be sure of it all without him writing the story for me. That would be the easy way to do it, to divide this in half and have him say half, then me. The cheat's way would be for me to take on both halves and *pretend* I was he.

Kazuo was standing by the Giant Panda in Ueno station. I saw him from a distance, turning his head from side to side, searching for me. I was still early – my feet fumbled and didn't move easily. A stall was selling soft rice cakes with all kinds of fruit inside, apricot, strawberry, plum, and keeping my head down low so he would not see me I bought some of these, something to hand over so it would not all be words.

He had written that he found it easier to contact me than his other friends, he found it easier to write of his loneliness to me.

He had drawn a sketch of the wall between himself and the employees who had been to University, who were already attending meetings that he was not asked to attend. Already he had lost hope of winning one of the three college places that the company sponsored each year.

I put my hand on his shoulder and handed him the cakes. I tried to understand. His hands were shaking a little, and his eyes flicked down to the cakes and up again.

'What now?'

We crossed the road and went into the park, past the steps where I had sat nearly a year before, one evening, watching, wondering how it was going to be. Then, a young woman had come to sit beside me, a student of conducting. She had given me a bell as big as a finger nail twisted round with coloured silks, and a golden loop to dangle it from, and she was pleased that I would remember it as my first gift ever from a Japanese person. She had said I would be given many more gifts over the year, and yes, I had lost count of them all months before. I had accepted gifts which I had handed straight on to someone else who was owed one, and this was quite a usual thing, not at all something to feel bad about. But I had carried the little bell with me, and even now it was in my wallet beside the disc of shiny metal.

I imagined the bell hanging on a Christmas tree in a future with people who would need such things, perhaps, to reach into this part of my life and share it with me. It was a word which felt into the past, in the way that an heirloom might.

Kazuo always carried with him a pen-knife which his father had given him, and when he was thinking of other things he often cleaned the dirt from under his nails with it, wiping the grey crescents by drawing the blade between his finger and thumb, then sprinkling the crumbs on the ground as he might sprinkle salt on food, delicately, without thinking. He was given the pen-knife for not telling his grandparents that his mother shouted at his father and his father shouted at his mother.

We passed the old woman who sold animals made from *kimono* scraps. Red and blue horses, yellow whales, a pink giraffe and flowered fish, jostled on the cloth laid over the pavement – ready for their next life, off the Ark.

Sometimes we walked too close together, sometimes too obviously far apart. We walked in circles – then took a train, straight through the suburbs, out, away from Tokyo, away from the wires that crossed the sky and kept the people netted to the streets.

There was a small red lacquer bridge reaching over the stream here, a red that cut and made brighter the green of the trees and the moss-covered stones below. We walked down from the road, and balancing on these stones we passed along the stream, Kazuo bowing his head although he could have walked straight under with room to spare. We could no longer hear the voices of people on the road, but only the running water, the leaves shifting above us, and birds. We sat so that we could not hear even our own footsteps.

'Are you happy?' He looked at me, and I nodded. 'I don't know why I'm so happy, but I feel so.' He paused. 'Do I seem young to you?'

'You don't seem young or old.' And then stupidly I added, 'Just right.'

'What do you mean?' I didn't know what I meant, not really.

'I'm not being fair, I'm sorry. For a moment it just seemed perfect, that's all.'

A bird hopped across the stones, and reaching the stream it jumped forward, beating the water into a shower around it. The wet from its feathers reached us. And then, half-washed, half-drowned, it staggered up and away.

'Why *did* you come?'

I replied feebly that I did not know, but I had told him this before, I was sure. I did not know if he meant from Sendai or England.

'You make friends all over the world, and what then?'

I thought for the hundredth time how all the places I had been to were like jars, one for each country, each lonely excursion, lined up on a shelf. Sometimes they were everything – the people, the places, the thoughts – they were what I was, but sometimes they were just jars of colours like glittery sweets through which light filtered.

I could see things differently through them. I could stand back from them.

But they did not fit well together, I could not easily mix what was in one with what was in the next, so each I looked at separately. Like friends you see one at a time, and after a while you behave just a little differently with each and it feels like you can never bring them together because then – who would you be? There were years and seas and languages glassing these jars around.

I hoped this year would not bottle in on itself, that I could make it more than another glass jar in my mind. Already I was trying to distance some memories – I was trying to hold at arm's length one person – and this made it harder – like there was a genie who would out if ever anything was allowed to rise. These were the muscular memories. These were the pictures that were not even still, but charged onward through my head. The scenes I had spread before me in Kyoto, that had wrapped me up tight as a winding sheet. But they were a part of me. They could not be thrown out neatly. And fighting only made them stronger. Rather I would remake them. I was now remaking.

'I won't forget. This is a part of what, or where I will be.'

'I don't even like being in Tokyo, away from everyone,' he said. 'All my friendships are drying out like rivers with no water.' He laughed, mocking his image.

Sato sensei is my only friend, Mr Moriya had said once. And I had heard and pretended not to hear.

My only friend.

We hitched a lift up to the base of the Tempodai lookout, and caught the final cable-car of the evening – the old man in his official's suit and cap was on his way to collect the last passengers, but he said he would take us up and bring us down again when he came to clear out the dustbins.

The light was faded but the lake which lay across the top of the mountains ahead had gathered to it the last sunlight and was golden. A long thread of water came from it, dropping down the cliff below like a ribbon leading up to the land which time forgot. Further down a small waterfall sprang from the rock face, a puncture.

Gradually the gold thinned away and the mountains and lake, waterfall and sky became a series of greys, as it must have done for the monk, hundreds of years ago, who had climbed up here, remembered the scene, and traced it in his inks on returning home so that every day he could travel into the space before us and forget himself.

We walked along the path for a short distance, following the crest of the mountain which sloped steeply on either side, and we could see the complicated lights of Nikko to our left and the huge, simple forms of mountains and lake, now dim, to our right. The old man called us through the dark, and we helped him heave the rubbish sacks onto the cable-car. He asked me to press the red button for going down.

The youth hostel was full – Kazuo could go back to his dormitory in Tokyo but I had nowhere to go, the last train for the north had left. We walked through the empty streets, passing the bobbing red lanterns strung outside the restaurants, listening to the voices within. We walked hesitantly – in the dark it seemed stranger that we were together like this – for being tired we could hardly communciate through words, and the darkness took our eyes and our hands away, so we did not know how to be. Or we did, but it was so impossible that it made us seem even further apart.

'You'd better get on back,' I said. 'I'll find somewhere.' But everywhere we had tried had been full.

'I can't leave.'

We took a taxi back over the Tempodai and up to the shore of the lake, to the tourist resort. I did not want to come here, to see the lake so close, but it did not touch the earlier memory, it was like another lake altogether. There were swan- and shark-shaped pedalos resting tied up to the banks, and stalls sold chocolate-dipped bananas sprinkled with gaudy hundreds and thousands. I bought a box of cheap bean cakes with a tasteful strip of bamboo across it, as *omiage* for the staffroom, but when I showed it to Kazuo he laughed kindly and said it was the one thing in the shop which was not Nikko-specific and therefore the gift was more or less meaningless. There was now no proof I had been here.

An old inn by the side of the lake was also full, but from it we could see in the distance bright lights in the shape of a deer surrounded by a flashing heart – a love hotel. Our walking had become very heavy, but we did get there and read the swinging sign under the deer's belly, and read that there were spaces.

'It will be cheap,' Kazuo said, biting the sides of his nails. And there was not really any choice. And I did not want to stay alone.

'Are you thinking of staying too?'

'In the same room?' He sounded so confused – we were walking as if on ice across the lake now, wanting to see just how far we would go. And then we were in the room together.

I think in any other room something different might have happened, but it chilled us and made us laugh at the same time, and then we knew we had fallen into the lake and were simply friends again. Before us there was a white plastic sofa which would do for one of us as a bed, and there were plenty of lacy blankets and one clammy sheet each. We flicked through the mail order catalogue for a company specialising in vibrators, one in the shape of Basho, one of Date Matsamune who was the founder of modern Sendai. An ancestor of Mr Moriya's had served under Matsamune, and Mr Moriya liked to think there was a blood relation between the men, in the not too distant past. I wondered whether he would have seen this little statue as a humiliation, or as an acknowledgement of power, of fame.

The wall paper had tiny rose buds on, all pointing the same way – regiments of rose buds marching up the wall – but from a distance they looked more like cockroaches.

The jacuzzi in the bathroom was disappointing, and dribbled through its holes as if it was crying. I called to Kazuo that we should have slept outside and showered under the waterfalls, but he did not answer.

When I came back to the bedroom he had fallen asleep on the sofa. I put a blanket over him and his heavy shoes stuck out from beneath the frilly edging.

The ceiling was padded like a nylon quilt, so that if you jumped on the bed and reached too high you could not hurt your head. I wanted to jump, but did not feel like doing this alone, it seemed the kind of thing one needed company for. After a while I stood up to touch it – I must have been feeling suspicious – I did not even notice I had risen until I felt the hardness against my fingers, for although it looked like padding there was lumpy plaster underneath the nylon gauze. I could see through a little tear, and the plaster felt cold. Soon after that I fell asleep.

'I don't think we need to go just yet.'

'It's starting soon.' He shifted his feet.

'No one else has gone yet.' I didn't move, and he sat down again.

But then, once the meeting was in progress, once we were sitting in the hall listening to the Headmaster drone on reassuringly about the plans for the new buildings, I saw him slip out from between his papers the flimsy red exercise book. The book I was supposed to have been chronicling my year in.

He passed a note.

How have I been as a supervisor this year:

a) publicly

b) privately?

Please write answer in book. With as much detail as possible.

I turned the paper and sent it back.

WHY?

He added,

It is good to learn from experience.

I wrote that I'd do it later, that I was not sure what he meant. And when later came, five minutes after returning to the staffroom, he explained,

'Of course, it is important to let me know, so that if we get another foreign teacher in the school I will know how it was for you.'

He sounded reasonable, but the problem was his voice did not sound reasonable at all. And his eyes looked crazy.

I stared at the blank page. I could have written all this down then. I could have written a treatise on power and on game-playing, or I could write, oh, you were a fine supervisor, intelligent, witty, charmingly original – all an English girl could wish for.

It looked so simple. Already it was crowded long before I touched it with the pen. But also it was simple.

I held my hand close to the paper, knowing I could write everything or nothing, or any little part I chose. It was not power now, it was strength. It was ordering, transforming, forming. There was no blame here.

I knew he was watching me from out the corner of his beady eye. He was not turning his pages, in that so-familiar way he had. The clock was ticking, noisily, and the deputy headmaster grunted as he slept. There was the sound of some teachers playing *go* in the smokers' corner, waiting for their next class. The counters clicked.

I touched the paper and wrote, hearing a breath of relief close to my right elbow.

You taught me a lot about Japan, and about England, and about myself. It is rather strange to be close to someone for this long, and then to get up and leave one day and probably never seen them again. I feel confused at the moment [I was not sure if this was true, but it was a slippery term and would do] and I don't think I can really write what you want.

If you have another foreign teacher, I think the most important thing is that they get to know all the other teachers in the school earlier than I did. Perhaps I was too unsociable for the job. It is good to talk to a variety of people, and it is the only way this foreign teacher lark will really work.

I thought he would have fun working out what I meant. I closed the book and pushed it across the line between our desks, with a peace-smile, hoping it would do.

O n the final day of term an enormous box, big enough to fit a chair inside, turned up on my desk. In the envelope stuck to the top was a card with a sprig of cherry blossom on it, and inside was written, 'from Watanabe sensei to Anna sensei, with fond memories'.

Inside the box were four furry white cats, larger than ever a cat was in real life. A mother and kittens.

'You won't be able to take them, will you?' said Mr Moriya smugly. 'People have no idea what to give travellers.'

'Oh, I don't know,' I smiled, knowing full well that I would take them straight to Aki's children. It was strange to think I had never even told him about Aki's children.

He said that I must spend my last night at his home, in his daughter's room. He would have his wife prepare all my favourite food. Something about his voice, his tone, made me stiffen and fight still. I do not know why.

'Really, I would like to spend the last night in my own room,' I said. I wanted above all to be free, to wander, to say goodbye slowly to the town.

'That will not be possible. I have asked for your water to be switched off already.' He looked straight at me, noting my anger.

'That's fine,' I said, staring straight back.

I sat on the floor in my empty room.

I seemed to have been unloading objects for weeks – the pink futon with the little stain I had sent off with the big rubbish at last – my television was sold to James, who wanted a second one – he was gathering such things in order to persuade his parents-in-law-to-be that Sayoko and he needed a home of their own. Christobel had my deluxe futon, Aki all my kitchen things, and the pink rice-cooker which the Headmaster had given me soon after my arrival.

The rains were almost over, and everything was clean. From my window I could just see the river, bulging at its concrete banks. The real heat was expected any day.

My refusal to stay with Mr Moriya seemed unreasonable now. Ridiculous.

I went to Aki's house. Grandfather videoed us all eating supper, so everyone was well-behaved – Jun did not bark for more rice, but helped himself to it. If we said something witty, we were told to repeat it again, facing the camera in case the words hadn't come out clearly. Now and then Jun said, 'Please, Father, we are not film stars,' but the old man continued his director-ship, sweetly oblivious.

I thought of Kazuo and his moving portraits, and the morning in Nikko when I woke up and found him sitting beside me, with tea just made.

'I'm sorry about last night,' he had said.

'Why?'

'I should not have stayed, and I should not have gone to sleep.' He laughed.

I held out my hand to him and touched his fingers.

'I think we did the right thing.'

'You are not angry?'

I asked him why I should be angry – of course I had not been angry. I was not sure, though, what he meant.

'I saw you touch the ceiling,' he hesitated.

'That's okay,' I said. It didn't make any difference either way.

'I opened my eyes and you were stretching upwards – it was strange.'

'I liked putting the blanket over you.' I hoped this did not sound too foolish, this ordinary thing out of place.

We had breakfast together near the station, and then I went back to Sendai on the fast train and he got the local express into Tokyo. We decided not to contact each other again before I left, and he said he would write to me in England.

Aki was going to send me some of her stories, and I got Jun to promise he would add a few old poems too. They said they would come to England some day, and perhaps we might even go up Snowdon together, singing.

'Oh goodness, I forgot those stones from Zao,' I said with a silly giggle. 'I wonder where they got to?' Ichiro's face lit up – I think these were the first words I had said which he had understood, and for once I too understood him clearly.

'You can have some of *my* stones,' he smiled, first at me, then straight into the lens of the camera.

He came with me to the apartment, which was now completely empty but for some small boxes and my suitcase. He had not been here since I first arrived. He never saw it as it was when it was mine. Yoshimoto sensei had come to help me clean up, and she had taken the mirror for her daughter's bedroom, her daughter whom I had never met. Mr Moriya had offered to send his wife along, but I said we two would manage fine by ourselves.

He helped me take the boxes to the post office, and as a reminder of old times he caused utter havoc, tying himself in knots with the tape, and somehow succeeding in getting himself attached to one of my parcels. The nice post office man whom I knew now laughed silently with me and whispered, 'How would you like him to go back to England with you?' Not greatly, I replied.

I felt very distant from him already.

I dragged the suitcase down the stairs, and the wheels clicked sharply at each step, like a timer. The taxi motor was burring.

He clasped my hand tightly, as if he was clinging to a rock in a wild sea.

Maybe I did love him.

'Will you kiss me?' he asked. 'Can we say our farewell the European way?' He was smiling, and his glasses reflected the light, so I wasn't sure, but he had tears I thought.

I leant upwards, and kissed his cheek, which was a bit damp – and then with his hands he grasped the sides of my chin and fumblingly pulled me to his lips, and blindly – thoughtlessly, for it was nothing to me now – I jerked my head back as if he would strike me.

We stood facing each other, and the taxi-driver watched but we did not notice him. Then I bowed my head and took a step backwards, sideways, opened the car door.

'I'd better go,' I said, wiping my wet lips. 'Thank you. Thank you for everything.'

'Remember me, Anna sensei,' he called, clasping his hands together, and I was not sure if I was being fooled one last time, because surely his tragedy was ending just as he knew all along it would end, and therefore I was doing nothing I needed to feel bad about. But I did feel bad. He wrung his hands with zest as we turned the corner, and we drove along the school fence and past the chained gate, in silence. Then the driver said,

'I expect he was a good friend while you lived here.'

Epitaph

I went up a hill round the back and slipped down under cover of the trees. There was rubbish around – plastic bags had drifted up, and tin cans had come down. Voices got nearer. I reached the back of the toilets, strolled round the stinking wall, and arrived in the compound as crooked-looking a thief as any in striped shirt. But no one noticed me.

We waited for the geyser. It was about to perform, and some people were getting a bit restless holding up their cameras. The guide was apologetic.

Then in a rush the water came. I have a diagram of the caverns that it travelled through, but I do not believe in it. There is no light down there, just shapes, just feeling.

The plume of water could have reached twice as high as the space it was allowed, but a stone arch had been built to frame it, so as the water hit the top it splayed out, spitting at us, ferocious as Rumpelstiltskin – incomprehensible and yet probably we all had some idea what it was saying. And then it withered back, and its wet – even the wet in our hair – began a downward descent, though some drops would have to go home via the clouds.

This was what I had come to see. And the thing I had come to do was bathe in sand.

There were four or five of us in a row, all naked and headed the same way.

An old woman came up to me when it was my turn and flashed her golden teeth in my face and pulled back my hair, her hands stretching out my neck, pulling the veins straight. She began pouring sand on my toes, and slowly she buried me, but each part she buried came to life, the opposite of Socrates.

I was awakened to the blood in me, to its rhythms, to the organs working mechanically which for the first time ever I could see. To my shape in the earth. I rather hoped she would cover my head but that would have been to see too much too early, so she patted the sand around my chin and left me.

I lay throbbing like a simple particle, and then, when the old woman bid me, I moved and the black sand cracked from head to foot, and my limbs appeared, and I rose.